My Own
Lightning

My Own Lightning

SEQUEL TO THE
NEWBERY HONOR WINNER
Wolf Hollow

Lauren Wolk

DUTTON CHILDREN'S BOOKS

DUTTON CHILDREN'S BOOKS
An imprint of Penguin Random House LLC, New York

First published in the United States of America by Dutton Children's Books,
an imprint of Penguin Random House LLC, 2022

Copyright © 2022 by Lauren Wolk

Visit us online at penguinrandomhouse.com.

Library of Congress Cataloging-in-Publication Data is available.

Book manufactured in Canada

ISBN 9780525555599

10 9 8 7 6 5 4 3 2 1

FRI
Edited by Julie Strauss-Gabel
Design by Anna Booth
Text set in Harriet Text

For my sisters,
Suzanne Jane Wolk and Cally Robyn Wolk.

And for our grandparents,
Ann and Fred McConnell,
whose farm was such an important part of our lives.

Western Pennsylvania

1944

CHAPTER ONE

I didn't know there was a storm coming.

Had I known, I might have done things differently.

But I'd promised to help my teacher, Mrs. Taylor, clean the schoolhouse before she locked its doors for the summer.

So I made my way up the lane from our glen to the top of the hill, past Toby's grave (though I stopped for a moment to lay my hand on his headstone), down again through a field of young wheat, and into the woods of Wolf Hollow.

The trees themselves were friendly enough, and the sunlight filtering through their leaves tried its best to cheer me up, but the path through the hollow awakened dark memories I'd tried to put to rest. Memories that never slept soundly and were apt to startle like birds at the smallest twitch, rising as they woke, while I fell deeper and deeper into gloom.

Just months before, I'd tried to save my friend Toby from a girl named Betty. She, a bully through and through. He, a ruin of a man who made an ample target for a girl practicing her aim. Both of them gone now, except for the marks they'd left on me. The marks I'd left on myself, trying to be of help.

Since Toby's death, I had been distracted by might-have-beens and if-onlys. Consumed with what I could have done differently. Not quite trusting myself as I once had. All of which laid me low. Especially when I walked through the woods that had once been Toby's home.

But Mrs. Taylor was waiting for me, her broom and scrub brush, bucket and mop ready for work, and I was glad to join her for a task that would set me straight again, face forward, my memories folding their wings and settling again in their nests where they belonged.

"And how is your summer so far, Annabelle?" Mrs. Taylor asked as she polished dust and stove-soot from the windowpanes.

June was an odd time: school was out—which meant a pause in my most important job—but there was so much farmwork to be done that I was busier than ever.

"It's been fine," I said, sweeping up boot-mud and dried bits of nimblewill. "Lots of planting to do. Strawberries to pick." She didn't need to be told. Most of us in the township were farmers. Everyone knew what that meant. "But I love being outside. So."

She nodded.

We worked on in easy silence, the schoolhouse strange without the squeak and shuffle of children at every desk and the patter of Mrs. Taylor huddled with one small cluster after another up at the chalkboard, the smell of warm bag lunches: meat sandwiches, oily cheese, a whiff of boiled egg.

Instead, we shared a silence punctuated only by the squeal of newspaper wetted with vinegar that Mrs. Taylor was using to clean the windows. The *hush, hush, hush* of my broom. And then, unexpectedly, a knock at the door.

Mrs. Taylor looked at me and I at her.

"Who on earth?" She climbed down off her stepladder and went along quickly to find out who had come and why.

I followed her, standing back a little but able to see that there was a man on the stoop. Past twenty but not yet thirty. Someone I'd never seen before.

I would have called him handsome, but he wasn't. He was beautiful.

"Can I help you?" Mrs. Taylor said, wiping her hands on her apron.

"I hope so." He smiled, his teeth even and white.

He had a well-trimmed mustache, though no beard— which was unusual in these hills, where the two usually went hand in hand—and green eyes, my favorite kind. A big man, especially across the shoulders, with a barrel chest, like a lumberjack. Except he was dressed more like someone from town, in clean, tidy clothes, his cuffs buttoned, the kind of hat my father wore to church.

The word *gentleman* came to mind, but his eyes were curiously flat, and I had a vague suspicion that he might not be quite what he seemed. Perhaps he'd been in the war and was still finding his way all the way back from that. Or—

"I'm looking for my dog, Zeus," he said, and I relaxed.

I liked people who liked dogs.

"My name is Graf. From Aliquippa. Far enough so I doubt you'll see Zeus around here. But I've been looking for most of a week, and I guess I'm grasping at straws." He made a small, helpless gesture with one hand.

"What kind of dog?" I asked.

"A bull terrier. Brown. With a white patch on his shoulder."

"I'm sorry," Mrs. Taylor said, "but I haven't seen a dog like that. Have you, Annabelle?"

I shook my head. "Lots of dogs around here, but not one like that. I'd remember."

"Well, let me know if he turns up." Mr. Graf pulled a strip of paper from his pocket and held it out. "Here's my telephone number."

Mrs. Taylor took it and slipped it into her apron pocket. "Of course we will."

It seemed that we were all done, Mrs. Taylor raising her eyebrows as if to say, *Was there something else you wanted?*

But I saw no need to hurry. Looking at him was like looking at a painting or a flower garden, and I hadn't yet had my fill.

"I'll ask my brothers to keep an eye out, too, Mr. Graf," I said.

"Call me Drake." He smiled at me, and I felt taller. Older.

"Like the duck?" I said . . . and I immediately felt small again. Young. "Not that you look like a duck. In fact—"

"Never mind that," Mrs. Taylor said briskly. "We'll be in touch if we see your dog, Mr. Graf."

"Good." He hesitated. "I wouldn't recommend that you try to put a leash on him. Zeus isn't very . . . comfortable around strangers. Best just to call me if he turns up."

I wondered about that. About the word *comfortable*. Which could mean a few things.

And that name. Zeus. A Greek god. Which made the dog sound fearsome.

But dogs got their names when they were tiny and weak and blind, so I decided the name said more about Mr. Graf than it did about Zeus.

"Oh, and I'm offering a reward. Ten dollars," he said. Which was a lot of money.

I wondered why he had saved that piece for last, like a cookie.

If we had already found his dog and said as much without knowing about a reward, would he have given one? I thought maybe not.

But then I felt guilty for thinking ill of a man who'd done nothing wrong. I didn't like it when other people jumped to conclusions, so I tried not to do that myself, though it was hard sometimes. Knowing what to trust and what to doubt.

"That's a lot of money," Mrs. Turner said, her eyebrows up.

"Zeus is a lot of dog," Mr. Graf replied, smiling his white smile.

I watched as he tipped his hat and turned toward his truck, which was parked along the edge of the dirt road that led through Wolf Hollow and out, eventually, to the hardtop and on toward places like Aliquippa with its gas stations and coffee shops and beauty salons and all the other things we didn't have in our hills.

Compared to such places, the glen where we lived was like a cradle.

"You can always go visit somewhere else," my father liked to say, "but then you get to come home."

So far, home had been plenty.

But as Mrs. Taylor and I watched Mr. Graf pull away, a part of me wanted to see what else there was to see.

"He must really love his dog to go driving around the countryside like that," Mrs. Taylor said. "And to offer such a big reward!"

"He must," I replied.

And then, just before she shut the door, I caught sight of a boy on the other side of the road, a bit down from the schoolhouse, standing in the tall weeds, watching us.

Despite the trees casting shadows along the road, despite the way he had pulled his hat down low over his forehead, I knew who he was.

Andy Woodberry.

"What's he doing here?" Mrs. Taylor said, and I could hear that she was frowning.

"I don't know. He's hardly ever in school when he's supposed to be, but now it's June and here he is."

Mrs. Taylor responded by closing the door and, with it, the subject.

But I stayed where I was for a long moment, wondering what had brought Andy this way. There was nothing much along this piece of road except the school and, a bit farther down toward the flatland, our old potato house where we stored the crop until we could sell it. A distance beyond that: the Woodberry farm. Where Andy should have been.

But Andy wasn't my business anymore. And I was not his keeper.

So I bolted the door and turned back to my work, Mrs. Taylor wondering out loud about Mr. Graf and his missing dog, both of us eager to finish up and be on our way home.

I decided I would tell everyone about Mr. Graf and Zeus at dinner that night, in case they met either one.

The reward money would be nice. Finding a lost dog would be even nicer.

As I swept and dusted, I imagined saving Zeus. Taking him home to Mr. Graf. How good that would feel: to do something right. With no mistakes. No might-have-beens.

And that was when I heard the first roll of thunder in the distance.

"Was that thunder?" Mrs. Taylor asked, peering through the window. "We could certainly use the rain."

I joined her, looking out at a sky still blue.

"Maybe I ought to hightail it on home," I said as the thunder sounded again, still as mild as gravel in a bucket, though perhaps a bit closer this time. "Before it gets here."

Mrs. Taylor looked at me doubtfully. "Do you think you'll be all right?"

"I'll run," I said. "I'm sure I'll beat it home."

But I hadn't reckoned on the speed of that storm, or how easily it would cross the distance between us.

CHAPTER TWO

By the time I had climbed up out of Wolf Hollow to where the woods ended, the storm had come stomping out of the west in its big black boots, gnashing its teeth and shouting itself hoarse, and I realized that I shouldn't have ignored the maple leaves that had flashed their white warnings or the wind as it had suddenly blown cold against my bare arms.

But I *had* ignored them, and now I was caught unprepared, without so much as a hat on my head.

I knew about storms. I knew not to stand under a tree. I knew to stay away from anything metal, anything tall. I knew that if I could hear thunder, I was within reach of lightning.

But I was nearly home, with no shelter to be had, and the thought of lying flat on the ground to wait out the worst of it seemed idiotic. So I hurried on just as the storm pulled a fistful of cold, wet marbles from its pocket and flung them against my face.

In the space of a moment, I was drenched, heavy with rain, torn between wanting the shelter of the trees and knowing I should leave them.

It was the lightning itself that made me run, though I crouched at every white flash—as if the storm were taking my picture—and then raced on, fast as I could.

When I reached the crest of the hill where the lane waited to lead me down again toward home, I paused, shocked at the sight of the hemlocks along the lane thrashing and twisting like they were trying to pull up their roots and run.

I was standing there, rigid with fear, when suddenly the air fizzed around me, as if I'd been dipped in wasps.

In an instant, those wasps stung me all at once, every inch of me, inside and out, and I knew nothing at all except a sizzling pain in my head, a dreadful heat, a sharp emptiness in my chest, and a kind of ending.

Someone started me again.

From a dark and distant place, I felt someone pounding on my chest, again and again, and I thought of my mother punching down a great white belly of dough.

I opened my eyes, hoping to see her, but found myself in a curious night, impossibly dark, as if the stars were all inside my head.

The pounding stopped.

I felt a rough hand on my cheek.

Suddenly—the cold rain, though it had surely been falling all along. The deep, disturbing thud of thunder in every one of my bones.

And then I slipped away again.

When I woke, I was being carried.

Not gently. At a run. I still couldn't see anything, and my thoughts were clogged with mud and old straw, better suited for a swallow's nest than a girl's head.

But I could smell the rain as I'd never smelled it before: both clean and tarnished, like hot metal and plowed dirt and pond rot all mixed together.

And then I was inside. In my own home. I knew it from the smell of bleach and bread but also, for the first time, from other things, too: the chalky white mineral crust around the sink spigot, the vaguely rotten stink of the gas stove, and especially the slop bucket, full of tattered cabbage leaves and coffee grounds.

And I knew it from the smell of the people. Their end-of-the-day sweat. A sweetness that brought to mind my grubby little brothers. A sourness that was, perhaps, the scent of my grandmother, who was unwell.

What's happening to me? I thought as I heard my mother say, "Lay her there," in a voice ragged with fear.

I wanted to tell her I was all right, but my own voice was still trying to find its way back.

"What's wrong with her?" my grandma said. She sounded as if she were crying, which choked me, too, and made me cough, which loosed from my aunt Lily a quick bark of prayer.

I knew I was on the big tiger oak table in our kitchen where I'd been laid out once before after I'd stumbled into a nest of yellow jackets. My mother had daubed me with wet baking soda until I was as speckled as a fawn.

Even over the thunder, I could hear my little brother James yelling, "Annabelle!" over and over. "Annabelle, wake up!"

Which was when I began to see again.

Just a little light at first, and then, more quickly, the shapes of people, the color of them, their faces all around the table looking down at me, like the petals of a flower.

As my sight cleared, everything became sharper and sharper . . . and then went past what I'd always seen before, past ordinary, to colors that were brighter, everything edged in light.

My mother, leaning over me, must have seen that same light reflected in my eyes.

"Oh, there you are," she murmured, trying to smile, her hand on my cheek, which took me back to the top of that hill. To the memory of that other, rougher hand.

She closed her eyes and let out her breath.

"It must have been just a glancing blow," my father said, his hand on my pulse. "Her heart's good and steady."

"But look at this!" My mother lifted my right arm, and I could see a frenzy of red burns that ran across my skin like a lightning-vine. *"Dear Lord."* She laid my arm gently down again.

"I called Dr. Peck," my father said, smoothing the hair off my forehead, "but his wife said he's over in Coraopolis, delivering a baby." He leaned closer. "Can you hear me, Annabelle?"

I nodded. I could hear him too well, in fact, as if he were shouting, though he wasn't.

My father felt for my pulse again. "Can you sit up?"

With some effort, I could.

"Then we'll wait for him to come." My father tried for a smile. "He'll have you good as new in no time."

"There would be no need if you hadn't gone out in the storm in the first place, Annabelle," Aunt Lily said, and I wanted to smack her. "I thought you were smarter than that."

But smart often comes *after* a mistake.

That was one lesson I'd already learned more than once.

I reckoned I'd learn it again, but I didn't foresee the other mistakes that were coming, or what other kinds of smart I'd become.

CHAPTER THREE

I'd once been shocked pretty badly, when I was ten, helping my father with wiring that should have been dead. And I would always remember how it had felt when the electric current ran up my arm. Like a warm, metallic hum in my veins. Something coppery on my tongue.

And then my father had shoved me away with his shoulder.

"Never grab a person with your hands if they're being shocked," he said later. "The shock will spread and make your hands grip harder, so you can't let go. Always use something wood to break the connection. Never metal. Or, if you must, make sure to knock the person free with a part of yourself that won't grip."

"Like your shoulder." I rubbed the place where he'd shoved me.

"Or a fist."

I remember thinking how odd that was: punching someone to help them.

As I lay in bed that night, trying to come all the way back from where I'd been, my mother dozing in a rocker nearby, I realized that someone had saved me this time by punching my heart awake.

My mother saw the bruises on my chest as she helped me get dressed the next morning. Ugly blue-and-green blotches, nothing like the red burns that unfurled like fiddleheads all along my arm.

"What are those bruises?" she asked me, wide-eyed. *"Annabelle, who did this to you?"*

But I couldn't answer. The words waited, but they were in no hurry.

I stared at her, trying to make sense out of the jumble in my head. Trying to snap myself properly awake.

But while the rest of the world marched on at its usual quick pace, I was living in slow motion, like I'd been slapped hard and was still stunned.

Only my senses were fully alert. I could smell everything from the Fels-Naptha soap my mother used on stains to the scorched ruins of my shirt, draped over the foot of my bed. And I could hear every footfall, the sound of my grandmother humming to herself in the kitchen below, the wail of a freight train, though the nearest tracks were miles away. And I could feel even the slightest touch, how the stitching on my clothes lay on my skin like tiny chains.

I felt as if I were inside a kaleidoscope, full of bright, colorful puzzles, and I was both fascinated and alarmed by what was happening to me.

"Annabelle?" my mother said, her face pinched with worry. "Did you hear me? Do you know where those bruises came from?"

But when I still didn't answer, she grabbed me in her arms. Kissed the top of my head. "It's all right," she murmured. "We'll sort everything out. Just go easy now."

And she helped me brush the weird, frizzy clumps from my hair, and then held my hand as we made our way slowly down the stairs to the kitchen.

"Well, there's our girl," my grandpap said from his spot at the table. He smiled at me, but I could see the worry in his eyes.

My grandma put down her coffee cup and reached out an arm. "Come here, child, so I can get a good look at you." Her heart was bad, and she now lived from chair to chair, else she would have come bustling to my side, all plump arms around me, all soft cheek against mine.

She pulled me into a half hug and murmured "*Thank you*" into my ribs, though I knew she wasn't talking to me.

"I bet Annabelle has superpowers now," James said.

"Like maybe she can shoot lightning bolts out of her fingers."

My other brother, Henry, who was a couple of years older than James, huffed at that. "Why would she want to shoot lightning bolts out of her fingers?"

"What a foolish question," James said.

"What a foolish boy," Henry replied. "Your superpower seems to be shooting nonsense out of your mouth."

My father said, "Boys," in a stern voice, but I could see that he was trying not to smile.

And I would have smiled, too, but I was too far away, too deep inside my own skin, though I noted with interest that Henry seemed oddly grim, almost angry, as he sat at his breakfast that morning.

My grandpap gave me an answer to that when he said, "Still no sign of Buster?"

Henry shook his head.

Buster was Henry's dog. A beat-up stray who'd arrived two months earlier on Easter morning when no one expected anything beyond church and a dinner of ham and scalloped potatoes, applesauce and cinnamon, warm buttermilk biscuits, the first of the asparagus tasting like spring.

There had been other dogs on our farm, and we'd liked them all, but Buster was special, especially to Henry, and from that day forward, the two of them were paired and promised, like all best friends are, and never far apart, even on school days. Buster would sit outside the schoolhouse like a flop-eared sentinel, waiting for Henry to reappear. And he slept at the foot of Henry's bed despite Aunt Lily's protests, most of them having to do with mud and fleas and slobber (though Buster was remarkably tidy, for a farm dog).

And now, it seemed, he was missing. Just like Mr. Graf's missing Zeus, though I couldn't imagine one had anything to do with the other.

I wanted to ask what had happened to Buster, but the question in my head stayed there, stuck.

At the look on my face, Henry sighed. "He was out in that storm, too, though I don't know why, since he's a big chicken when there's thunder."

Like most dogs. Thunder and gun shot. Fireworks, too, though we had those but once a year.

"I went with Daddy to Ambridge to pick up some peck baskets," Henry said bitterly. "Buster was gone when we got back. I should have taken him with us."

I watched Henry. His bowed head. The sag in his shoulders.

I knew something about regret and was well aware of the should-haves of my own life. Well aware that there would be others.

Already had been.

Among them, my decision to try and outrun a storm.

"Eat up." My mother put my breakfast down in front of me. "Dr. Peck will be here any minute now."

I hoped he would be able to help me release what was stuck.

My voice, mostly. But questions, too.

The loudest of them: Who had brought me back to life? And why had they not stayed to say so?

CHAPTER FOUR

"She'll be fuzzy and out of sorts for a few days, but she'll talk again," Dr. Peck said as we sat in my room, me on the bed, him on a chair alongside me, my parents standing nearby. "I'm quite sure of it. When she's ready. Nothing wrong with her vocal cords," for I had made a sound when Dr. Peck pricked my foot with a needle. "Or her hearing," for I had answered his questions with a nod or a shake of my head. "Or her eyesight," for I had followed Dr. Peck's finger back and forth. "Her circuits are a bit scrambled." He frowned a little. "Lightning will do that to a person. But we'll see how it goes."

I didn't know much about a person's circuits, but I knew enough to ask the question that bothered me most. "Isn't my brain all circuits?"

And there I was. Back. Just like that.

I reckoned curiosity was a potent force, too.

My mother burst into tears. My father smiled.

"Well, that's a relief," the doctor said, though he'd been "quite sure" I'd speak again.

I cleared my throat and asked my question again. "Mrs. Taylor told us we run on electricity, like radios."

Dr. Peck answered with a frown and a waggle of his head. "Well, yes, Annabelle. We run on electricity, head to toe. Fortunately, the human body is a wondrous thing. Especially a child's body. It can repair many problems that ail it. As you yourself just proved."

"What about the burns on her arm?" my mother asked, drying her tears.

"Those are called Lichtenberg figures. Kerauno-graphic marks. Lightning flowers. Lots of names for something so simple. Yet so unusual." He lifted up my arm and peered at the burns. "They'll fade away in time." He looked into my eyes again, thoughtful. "Of greater concern is any deeper burn, to the muscles or the organs. But you seem to be all right, Annabelle. Unless there's something you're not telling me."

"Just that everything's louder than before," I said slowly. "Brighter. And everything smells and tastes so strong."

"Hmm. Well, more is better than less. So if that's all

you've noticed, I'd say you're one very lucky girl. The lightning barely grazed you, else you'd be in the hospital right now and facing months of recovery. Maybe years."

"Oh!" my mother said suddenly. "But those bruises, Annabelle. I almost forgot about those."

When I pulled down the neck of my shirt, Dr. Peck could see that I was black and blue.

"That's not from the lightning," he said, watching my face.

I looked from him to my parents and back again. "The lightning knocked me out cold. And I woke up when someone was punching me on the chest. He stopped when I opened my eyes."

They stared at me. "*He?*" my father said.

I thought about that. "I don't know. Maybe she. But I felt a hand on my cheek, and it was rough. Like yours," I said to my father. "So I thought *he*. I thought you . . . but it wasn't."

He shook his head. "I went searching for you when we got back from Ambridge, and I found you lying at the top of the hill." His face was pale with the memory of it. "I didn't know at first that you'd been struck by lightning."

"And something else, too," the doctor said. "Some*one* else. Though in a good way." He sighed through his nose. "Likely started your heart again. Saved your life."

I swallowed. "So I wasn't just knocked out?"

He shrugged. "Even if it doesn't do much other damage, lightning can easily stop a heart. Something has to get it started again."

When he left us, he told my mother to bring me in for a checkup in a day or two. "Just to make sure all's well."

Which split me evenly between the desire to go back to "all's well" and a building hunger to learn what was new about me.

Fighting Betty and losing Toby had taught me that nothing stays the same. And now the storm had proved it once again. In the blink of an eye, my world had tipped on its axis, but this time I was curious about the changes in me. A little scared but excited, too, by how I fizzed and crackled, as if I were still full of lightning.

I felt like I'd been given a chance to become stronger. Smarter.

Trying to save Toby had been my best deed, but the lies I'd told along the way had been my worst mistakes, and they were at the root of the what-ifs that now followed me through my days.

Perhaps, if I'd been full of lightning at the time, I'd have known more, understood more.

And maybe been able to save him.

CHAPTER FIVE

It was odd how everyone relaxed once I could talk again. As if the sound of my voice—the thing that came out of me—was a more important bridge than the things I took in: what I could see, or smell, or taste, or hear.

Had I been a castaway or a hermit, perhaps my voice wouldn't have mattered as much, though surely the things worth saying would have been of value, whether anyone heard them or not.

These were the thoughts that occupied me all during that first morning after I'd been struck.

It was my brother Henry who pulled me back from my musings and focused me squarely on something else.

"I've already searched nearby, calling and calling," Henry said when he came out to the peach orchard where I was redding up from the spring pruning, my father and my grandpap thinning the crop. "I looked in every henhouse, smokehouse, and barn from here to the church. But no Buster."

"He's not a hen," James said, sitting in a nest of weeds like a duck in a hat. "Or a ham. Or a cow. Why would he be in any of those places instead of right here?"

To which we had no answer.

If Buster could have been with us, he would have been.

Which meant he'd been hurt or taken or worse.

My grandpap shook his head. "He'll be back. Dogs wander sometimes and come home when they're ready. I've lost count of how many dogs have appeared on this farm over the years, out of nowhere. And how many have disappeared. Don't forget, Henry: Buster showed up here at Easter, on a wander."

Henry looked forlorn at that. "You think he's gone off again, hoping for a better home?"

"No better home than here. Than you," my grandpap said.

"I met a man yesterday, at the schoolhouse," I said, remembering. "Mr. Graf. From Aliquippa. He was looking for his lost bull terrier. Brown with a white patch on his shoulder."

"Mr. Graf was looking around here?" my father asked. "Aliquippa's miles away, even as the crow flies."

My grandpap shrugged. "As I said, a dog will wander."

"If anyone sees him, Mrs. Taylor has his telephone number."

James said, "I never heard of a dog with his own telephone."

"Mr. Graf's telephone." I tossed a twig at him. "And he's offering a ten-dollar reward."

"Ten dollars!" James yelped, his eyes wide. "That's enough for—"

"Shoes for all three of you," my father said.

"Aw, shoes." James hung his head sadly. "It's always shoes."

"Well, you've got to find the dog first, which won't be easy, though this one sounds a bit easier to place than some," my grandpap said. "Handy, to have a white patch on your shoulder, so everyone knows who you are."

He was using a long stick with a black rubber sleeve to knock some of the little peaches off their branches, one by one. Not many. Some farmers thinned their peaches by half or more so the ones that remained were as big as softballs. But we believed that bigger didn't necessarily mean better.

In years when frost hadn't blackened the buds, we thinned just enough peaches to ease the burden off the branches—which could break from the weight of a full crop—and let most of the fruit ripen in the sun, drink up the good rain, and mature into the best, most beautiful, most delicious peaches in the county, maybe the world. So juicy I had to bend at the waist when I ate one so I wouldn't stain my blouse. It seemed right, to bow like that, for peaches as fine as ours.

This early in the season, they were small and green and hard as shooter marbles, but I could still smell them all around me—a tight, sour tang that would need plenty of sun and rain and luck to make it sweet.

And I could hear the sizzle of bees zipping and buzzing among the clover at the far edge of the orchard.

And I could feel the sunlight burnishing my skin: it was heavier than usual, like a bright scarf on my shoulders.

I was glad for such fierce sensations, which brightened the gloom of the past few months, and I was tempted to hide in them, to let everything else look after itself so I could stay in this new layer of who I was.

But that's not all I was.

I added a branch to the pile I'd assembled. "I'll help you look for Buster, Henry."

"Well, maybe not quite yet," my father said as he reached his own long stick up into the tree. "In fact, you ought to be the one resting, and James, you ought to be gathering sticks."

But before I could answer, before I could tell him that helping find Buster would be the best of all medicines, Hunter—a quiet, lazy mutt (named for his surprising ability to catch groundhogs) who lived mostly in the rough but often kept us company while we worked—came plodding along the grassy lane between the rows of trees and flopped down in the weeds next to James.

Then he grinned at me, his tongue hanging out pink between the white spikes of his teeth.

And suddenly I felt calmer. Happier, as I ran my fingers through his fur, dust rising like a tiny brown storm.

Gone was the dark layer of worry I carried with me everywhere: the war that raged and raged across the world, the heart that ticked the hours away toward my grandma's end, the persistent ache that Betty and her terrible mischief had left behind.

The world suddenly seemed different. As if the trees had decided that green no longer suited them. As if, like Alice, I had entered a wonderland where I was taller than I'd ever been. A new girl altogether.

I went still, my eyes wide, and waited for an explanation. Looked at each of the others in turn, though they seemed the same as always, steady in their work. And then back at Hunter, who was still grinning at me, his eyes on mine.

It was the dog.

He was the reason I felt the way I did. Peaceful. Certain. Like a stone in the sun: solid and sure. All my thoughts round and whole, with no jagged edges.

Something I hadn't felt for some time.

How it this possible? I wondered, as amazed as a chick just come from her shell.

It felt like magic. Even more so because it was happening to me: an ordinary girl living in an ordinary place.

"*Is this how you feel all the time?*" I whispered, staring into Hunter's eyes.

"Is what how I feel all the time?" James said, trying to tie a bit of creeper to the dog's tail.

"I wasn't talking to you," I said, my eyes on Hunter.

I looked up to find Henry watching me, his face filled with curiosity.

"Are you all right, Annabelle?"

"Better than all right," I said. "I think I—"

But then Henry looked past me, and I turned to see a car coming down the lane, dust rising in its wake, to park at the end of the orchard.

We all watched as Constable Oleska climbed out of the car and headed toward us through the trees.

Hunter climbed to his feet and ambled off to a new nest a few trees away, leaving me unsettled again. Jagged and confused. Distracted again by the ordinary world. Some of it in the shape of Constable Oleska.

"Uh-oh," James said, moving to stand behind my father.

"What did you do, James?" Henry said.

"Nothing." But he stayed behind my father as the constable approached.

And I tucked my newest sense in among the others, like a flower in a bouquet, until I could see if it was just a daylily, blooming briefly and then gone. Or something likely to put down roots and stay.

CHAPTER SIX

Constable Oleska didn't wear a gun, but he was a big, stern man who looked like he didn't need one.

"Daniel," he said, nodding at my grandpap. "John," nodding at my father. "James. Annabelle. Henry."

"Constable," my father said.

Now that all our names were straight, James said, "Whatever got done, I didn't do it."

Which made the constable smile, though he didn't seem to be in a smiling mood. He turned to me. "I heard about the lightning strike. Happy to see you're in one piece."

I wanted to say *But I'm not. Not at all. Or if I am, it's a new piece. A whole new kind of piece.*

I wanted to tell him that the smell of his boot polish hurt my nose.

I wanted to tell him that there was a rip the size of an

eyelash in his shirt collar. That he'd missed a whisker when he'd shaved his chin that morning. That I could hear his belly growling from too much coffee, which had browned his breath and his teeth both.

"Someone thumped on her chest, left it all bruised," my grandpap said. "Got her heart started again. Leastways, that's what Dr. Peck says."

"Someone?" The constable watched me thoughtfully.

"I don't know who. But someone was there, pounding on my chest until I opened my eyes. I couldn't see, when I first woke up. But I knew someone was there. And next thing I knew, my daddy was carrying me home."

"A mystery hero." The constable chuckled. "Makes a nice change from a mystery hoodlum."

"No reason on earth to keep something like that a secret," my father said.

The constable shrugged. "People have their reasons."

James said, "Annabelle has superpowers now."

I almost laughed at the truth of it.

"Does she? Well, that's a blessing."

And I knew the constable was right.

He watched me for another moment before turning to my father.

He took off his hat, scratched the top of his head, put his hat back on. "I've come over to talk to you about Andy Woodberry."

Andy again. Twice in two days, after weeks without having to see his face or hear his name.

"What about him?" My grandpap sounded angry, and I really couldn't blame him.

Andy had always been something of a schoolhouse bully, teasing the smaller children, throwing snowballs at us in winter, putting burrs in our hair, that sort of thing. But until recently, he hadn't been any worse than some of the other older boys, and he wasn't in school often, working with his father instead, coming to school only to drowse by the woodstove when rain had turned the world to mud or the wind was cold enough to freeze his nose shut.

Then, last fall, Betty Glengarry had shown up and decided that he would be her . . . I wasn't sure what to call it. *Sidekick* sounded too jolly. *Stooge?* That made him sound like he hadn't known what he was doing when he helped her make such awful trouble for me, and Toby, and others, too. All of us, really.

Her *friend*, I guess. Andy had been her friend. And the worst parts of him had risen to the surface, bobbing and stinking in plain sight.

Once Betty was gone, we'd thought maybe Andy would lean back toward decent.

Instead, he'd been worse than ever. Mean. Sullen. Angry.

Whenever he'd looked at me, I'd seen such bitterness

in his eyes, though I didn't know how he could blame me for what had happened (even if I *was* sorry for the part I'd played).

I'd been relieved when he'd skipped the last few weeks of school altogether.

Mrs. Taylor had tried once or twice to get him back to his lessons, but she'd given up easily, and I knew she was happier with him gone. We all were.

Being stuck with Andy in the schoolhouse was a miserable business, but even passing by his farm was bad enough. If he was nearby, he'd stop what he was doing and stare at me. I could feel his eyes on me like sunburn.

It had been a while since I'd gone near his place on foot.

"I caught him living in your potato house," the constable said. "And I had a hard time believing you gave him permission."

My grandpap huffed. "Of course we didn't!"

"Well, but I did." My father sighed. "I caught him there myself, a couple of days ago, with a busted nose and nothing but the clothes on his back."

I tried to picture the scene: my father standing in the doorway of our old potato house, Andy huddled in a corner in his worn-out clothes, his face a mess.

I was surprised by what I felt as I imagined that. A dark sadness that Andy hadn't earned.

After what he'd done the year before, he deserved anger. He deserved disgust. And I felt plenty of both whenever I thought of him.

As I stood in the orchard, picturing him by Betty's side, I decided I wouldn't feel sad about his busted nose. Or where he slept, no matter where that might be.

I already had enough sadness.

And Andy deserved what he got.

"So you let him stay?" Henry said.

My father nodded. "Just until he could patch things up with his parents."

"His parents did that to him?" I asked. I knew they were hard people, but I hadn't known how hard, though I wasn't sure it mattered. Andy was hard, too, after all.

My father shrugged. "He claimed he stepped on a hoe blade and the handle snapped back, hit him in the face. But why leave home, unless home's where the problem lies?" He looked at the constable. "Maybe *that* deserves some of your attention."

The constable sighed. "I've had words with them before, John. No one's ever admitted to a problem. Not even Andy, as you said yourself, just now."

We all stood in silence for a long moment. Then, "Decent of you," the constable said. "To give him a place to stay for a bit."

"It's a potato house. Not much 'decent' about that."

"Better than nothing." He glanced back through the trees. "I put him in the patrol car, just in case."

My father raised his eyebrows. "For squatting in an old shed?"

Constable Oleska looked at me first and then back at my father. "Your Annabelle here knows something about small things that lead to bigger ones."

Which was true. Toby had looked like a villain, while Betty had looked like a posy—like something I could handle on my own—but she had turned out to have thorns. And trying to handle her had been a mistake.

My father rubbed his forehead. "Well, take him back to the potato house. Let him go."

I peered through the trees but couldn't see Andy where he waited inside the patrol car.

I wondered what he saw when he looked at me.

In April, a few days after Buster had shown up on our doorstep, we'd heard that Andy was missing his own dog, and we'd thought maybe Buster had belonged to him.

We could understand why a dog of his would decide to roam.

And we decided it was up to Buster to stay with us or, if he was Andy's dog, to go back.

He stayed.

But as I stood in the orchard that June morning,

watching the constable walk toward the patrol car, I said to Henry, "You don't think that's where Buster is, do you? With Andy?"

Henry shook his head. "Not by choice I don't."

I thought about that. "I don't know what we'd do if Buster was Andy's before he was yours, and Andy has him back again."

But Henry shook his head firmly. "Buster isn't Andy's. And he isn't mine. Buster is Buster's."

"It's like musical dogs around here," my father said, his eyes on his work. "Andy's mutt gone in April, Buster gone now. I can see why you might think there's a connection, Annabelle. And now a bull terrier. Though he's an Aliquippa dog."

"And nothing to do with Andy," I said. "But maybe we should ask him if he knows where Buster might be. And see what he says."

My father shook his head. "Not you, Annabelle. You were at the middle of all that business last fall. Andy remembers how you stood up for Toby when Andy himself tried to knock the man down. And you were the one who made us take a closer look at Betty. Even Andy, whether he'll admit it or not. And he's surely not over that yet. Maybe never will be." He sighed heavily. "I'm sure you remind him of a bad time and the worst of what he was."

"What he *is*," my grandpap insisted.

And part of me truly wanted that. To be a reminder of things Andy should never be allowed to forget.

Like helping Betty rig a sharp wire across the path that we traveled to school, the two of them pulling it tight between the trees so it stretched across just high enough to catch someone in the face. Or across the throat. It had caught James, our little James, across his forehead. Left him with a thin ribbon of scar.

Of all the bad deeds that Andy and Betty had done, that was one of the worst.

But another part of me suspected that Andy wouldn't have done such a thing on his own. That Betty had made him into a follower. Though he had made that decision himself, to do what he did.

It was confusing: how Andy could *decide* to be a follower. Which meant he *wasn't* a follower. Though he *was*.

"And now he's living in our potato house?" my grandpap said.

My father sighed. "No harm in showing the boy a little kindness. He hasn't had much of that."

"You get what you give," my grandpap replied.

There. What I felt exactly. I was even more sure of it, now that my grandpap had said so.

But my father had said something quite different, about kindness, and I wondered again what Andy saw as he sat waiting. As he looked at three generations of us there in that orchard together, surrounded by a world we'd built for ourselves.

I stared straight back toward him, but I couldn't see him at all from where I stood.

CHAPTER SEVEN

After the constable left, my father stayed behind with my grandpap to thin peaches while James told them how to do it, and Henry gathered sticks from the tall grass, and Hunter followed me down the lane to the house and my mother and more of a day I wouldn't soon forget.

When I got to the porch door, Hunter settled himself in the shade and put his head on his paws.

I knew, as surely as I'd ever known anything, that he would be waiting for me when I came out again.

"Good boy," I said, though the words seemed unnecessary.

I found my mother in the kitchen, at the sink, aproned, her hair in a kerchief, her hands busy with a chicken that had, just hours before, been chasing mice around the yard.

I could smell the chicken even from across the room:

a deeply meaty smell, its oily juices so fragrant I felt a bit like a fox.

"There you are," she said. "Are you all right, Annabelle?"

I nodded. "Just tired. A little wobbly. And my brain still feels fuzzy."

"Sounds like me on most mornings." She smiled. "But you tell me if anything worries you."

I was tempted to tell her about Hunter, but the list of things that were mine alone was pretty short, and I wanted this mysterious change to be just mine for a bit longer while I tried to figure it out.

Instead, I told her about Andy.

"He's living *where*?" my mother said.

"In the potato house. He had a fight with his parents."

She turned back to the chicken. "I think the lightning must have addled you more than you're letting on. Either that or your father's having some fun with you, Annabelle. He would never let that boy stay in our potato house after what he and Betty did last fall."

"The constable came by to say he'd caught Andy squatting there, but Daddy said it was all right, at least for the time being."

My mother picked up the trussed chicken and tucked it gently into a roasting pan. Then she carefully washed her hands, dried them on her apron, sat down at the kitchen table, and pulled out the chair next to hers. "Sit," she said. The *t* was as sharp as a carving knife, and I had a stray thought about blind mice as I sat down next to her.

She folded her hands in her lap, closed her eyes, opened them again, and smiled a small smile. "Your father is an interesting man."

I waited.

"He can do almost anything, fix almost anything, with little fuss. Even when no one taught him how."

I waited.

"He's strong and able and tough and honest and smart and has everything you might want in a person." She stopped to choose her words. "Including a soft heart, Annabelle. Which is a good thing. It balances out the rest of him and makes him more . . . interesting. Just right for me, really." She smiled again. "I wouldn't have done well with a hard-hearted man."

When she paused, I said, "He's a just-right father, too. But what does that have to do with Andy?"

She tipped her head. "Well, I wonder sometimes if people take advantage of that soft heart."

"You mean how Daddy lets Aunt Lily live with us even though she could live just fine on her own?"

My mother went still.

We both knew her life would be easier without Aunt Lily under the same roof.

"Never mind that," she said. "It's Andy I'm worried about at the moment."

I pictured him with Betty, sneaking around the hills and hollows, stirring up trouble for no reason at all. Or, if they'd had a reason, one I couldn't understand. Didn't want to understand.

I wasn't like Betty and Andy. Never would be.

"You mean if Daddy weren't so softhearted, Andy wouldn't have dared to sleep in our potato house?"

She nodded. "That's exactly what I mean."

I didn't think Andy should benefit from anyone's soft heart, but I didn't want my father's to be any harder than it had to be.

"Do you think it's worth the risk?" I said slowly. "To be a just-right person, even if people might take advantage of you?"

"That's the question, Annabelle." My mother stood up and smoothed her apron with her hands. "I think the answer depends on the size of the risk. And who you mean by 'people.'"

I thought about the answer as I helped my mother get lunch on the table—cold leftover pot roast glazed with jellied fat, a touch of homemade horseradish hot enough to stun an ox, all of it tucked into biscuits right out of the oven, served with a dollop of sour cream and a dish of cool applesauce—and then I rang the big front-porch dinner bell that called everyone to the table, all but Aunt Lily, who was at the post office where she worked, a bit too far for lunch most days, which was a blessing.

Aunt Lily tended to be a lot like the horseradish: best in small doses.

The bell was so much louder than usual that I let go of the rope and wedged my hands over my ears, watching the bell slowly swing itself down to a whisper.

As I stood there, mesmerized by the sound passing through my hands, I pictured Andy running from his home, his face bloodied and swollen. Pictured him heading down the straight road through the flat bottomland where we grew corn and potatoes. On to where the road sloped up into the trees, and a bit beyond to the potato house tucked into the cool shadows alongside the road, waiting for another crop to fill it up.

I pictured him stopping there. Finding a place to take shelter.

I hadn't been in the potato house for some time, but I could still smell the parched dirt–hot wood–dusty burlap–potato stain–mouse mess–tin roof of the place.

This time, when I pictured Andy sleeping there, I turned and went back inside my house, past the purple window in the front hallway, through the sitting room with its big fireplace and pictures of us on the walls, the breeze blowing the gauzy curtains into silent sails, to the kitchen, where the tiger oak table was set for us all, the boys coming through the door at speed, knocking their boots off into a dusty jumble and racing to their seats, my father and grandpap coming along more slowly behind them, hanging up their hats, my mother telling my grandma to *Sit, sit, everything's done*, and *James, Henry, hands!* Shooing them off to wash up. The smell of coffee hot in the pot and a strawberry pie on the counter. Plenty of sweet. Plenty of bitter. Enough of both for balance.

Just right.

From the doorway to the kitchen I watched all that. Saw more than I'd ever seen before.

And asked myself, again, if being a just-right person was worth taking a risk.

But then I pictured Andy with Betty on the path into Wolf Hollow, tying a sharp wire between two helpless trees, grinning and laughing as they worked.

And I wasn't sure of anything.

CHAPTER EIGHT

"What's with him?" my father said as he hitched the horses to the wagon that afternoon, pausing to watch Hunter make a clumsy leap into the flatbed at the back. "That dog never goes anywhere unless there's grub involved."

Hunter curled up on a muddle of old canvas in one corner.

As I watched, he blinked at me sleepily and closed his eyes.

"He likes us, is all," I said slowly. Though there was more to it than that. "Where are you going?"

"Down to find Andy. To have a talk." His face was grim.

I heard the reluctance in his voice.

"I'll go with you."

"I don't think that's a good idea." He climbed onto the wagon seat and picked up the reins. "Like I said before, the boy can't see you straight, Annabelle. When he looks at you, he sees what happened last fall."

"And when I see him, that's what I see, too. So we're even."

My father shrugged. "I suppose. But—"

"And why should I worry about what he thinks of me?"

"I didn't say you should. I just reckon he's more likely to be himself and talk to me if you aren't there."

"Be himself? Who else would he be?"

My father frowned at me. "Annabelle, you aren't acting much like your own self at the moment." He searched my face. "Are you all right?"

"Yes, Daddy. If Andy's uncomfortable around me, that's his problem. I'm not comfortable around him, either. But if you're going down to talk to him, I'm going with you."

My father paused, the reins hanging loose in his hands. "I hope you don't think you can fix him, Annabelle."

"Who said anything about fixing?" Maybe I'd once had such a notion—triggered by his bitterness, after Betty's death—but it had been a long time since that thought had crossed my mind. "Andy's not my friend. He'll never be my friend. I don't want to fix anything."

"Then why come along?"

"To look out for you!" I cried, the truth of it surprising us both.

"To look out for *me*?" he said, his eyes wide, smiling a little.

I looked at my boots. "Mother says you have a soft heart."

At which he chuckled. "Talk about the pot calling the kettle black."

"It's not an insult. It's a good thing. But I don't like the thought of Andy making hay out of it."

He sighed, the laughter gone. "Sometimes I worry that all that trouble with Betty and Toby and Andy has hardened your heart, Annabelle."

It was as if he'd hit me. The idea that I was hardhearted.

"It hasn't," I said in a small voice, my throat tight. "I promise, Daddy, it hasn't."

He nodded, his eyes on mine. "I hope not."

Being honest about Andy didn't make me hardhearted. I was sure of it. He'd done some terrible things. Why shouldn't I say as much? "And how is any of that my fault?" I asked my father.

He raised his eyebrows. "Who said anything about fault?"

"You said I was hard-hearted."

My father sat up straight. "I didn't. I said I *worried*

about that. And I never said you were to blame for what happened. Though you've made some mistakes, Annabelle, and you know it."

"From trying to help." But he was right. I had made mistakes, and I did know it. To my bones, I knew it.

"Nonetheless." He kept his eyes on me.

I climbed onto the wagon bench alongside him. "I won't get in the way. And I won't make things worse than they are."

"Two good *won't*s." My father slid over to make room for me. "Don't forget them."

Hunter, behind us, butted my arm until I turned and said, "You settle, boy."

Which he did, turning once, twice, before flopping again into his canvas nest.

My father looked from me to Hunter and back again. "I've never known that dog to take to anyone the way he's taken to you, Annabelle. And in the blink of an eye after what, two years he's been hanging around here?"

I reached back and gave Hunter a scratch on his head.

It was nice, how easy it was to please him.

James said, "Where are you going?" as he came through the door and down the back steps, Henry behind him.

"Just on an errand," my father said. "You boys help Grandpap in the orchard."

"How come Annabelle gets to go with you?" James said, scowling, his hands on his hips.

"Leave her alone," Henry said.

Which I liked, that Henry still had one foot in James's world but was edging closer to mine. Some nights, after James fell asleep, Henry would come find me to talk about nothing in particular, the talk itself the thing that mattered. Or just to say good night, as if it were important to punctuate the day with such an ending.

"I'll watch for Buster as we go," I told him, quite aware that whatever else was happening at any given moment, Henry was watching, listening, wondering where his dog had gone. "And tomorrow we can search farther out." I turned to my father. "Will you drop us near the bridge after we go to Dr. Peck's? So we can cover more ground?"

He nodded. "If he says you're okay for a long, hot walk."

Henry stepped back, pulling James with him, to give the horses room as they headed up the lane.

"I bet Hunter knows where Buster is," James said as we plodded past.

Which was something I hadn't tried. To ask one dog where another might be.

But I couldn't speak dog.

I could sense Hunter, much the way I could sense other things more easily since the storm. But what I felt was vague: a river of unformed notions, both the kind that come from the heart and the kind that come from the body. Like contentment and the smell of bacon frying.

Human language was something else. It was parsed out in small bits, each one with a job to do. Like *Where is Buster?*

To which Hunter had no answer.

I imagined the best—Buster tied up in someone's yard, with no way to say where he belonged. And I imagined the worst.

And then I tried to be more like Hunter: in that wagon, in that moment, my father by my side, the burns on my arm already healing.

CHAPTER NINE

My father and I shared a comfortable silence as we traveled along to where the road tipped down through Wolf Hollow and eventually led to a long flat strip of fertile bottomland that we called, quite naturally, the bottom. Here, along one edge, ran Wheeler's Run, a wide, shallow stream that chuckled as it flowed, childlike, not a care in the world. Where crayfish tiptoed through the bright, shallow current like fragile toys, nearly invisible against the pebbly bottom, foraging for worms and bits of rot.

Like Hunter, Wheeler's Run was happy to be exactly what it was.

My brothers and I liked the cool creek in summer and the flatness of the bottomland after so much time in the hills, but we were leery of the Woodberry farm—of Andy, mostly, though we knew enough to give his parents a wide berth, too.

So we stayed on our piece, happy to leave the farther

bottomland alone, especially since there was nothing much else out that way but one farm after another, none of them finer than our own.

And there was no road finer than the one my father and I traveled on that June day as we went in search of Andy to sort out how his life had come to overlap ours again.

Above us, the branches trimmed the sun so it lay in patterns on the road, a tawny ribbon of soft summer dust and worn-out stone, the whole day so perfect that the birds made up new songs about it as we passed by.

And I realized, as we rode along, that Hunter wasn't the only creature I knew better than before.

I knew the birds, too. Their endless caution, which I reckoned was a habit of all small animals: to watch for danger from every angle, through every moment of the day. Even as they sang.

And I knew the horses. Their patience. How solid and matter-of-fact they were, resigned to their work but eager for the pasture that waited at the end of their chores.

The realization made me eager to plunge into the woods, in search of chipmunks and garter snakes and red foxes. To know them in a new way, too.

All around me, the world whispered its secrets, and I felt myself listening harder than I ever had before.

But then, up ahead, I saw the potato house, mute as a stone. And I pulled myself back to why I'd come.

Until now, the potato house had always been only what it was: a wooden shack, empty at this time of year, the last of the potatoes tucked into our root cellar, nothing left here but old burlap bags scattered like the petals of a spent flower. A slew of field mice. Pale spider-curtains at the grimy windows. Other times, it was where we stored bushels of reds and whites, sometimes sweets, but mostly plain old russet potatoes that were good for baking, boiling, roasting, and mashing. Ordinary, but useful in almost any situation.

Now it was a place where we expected to find a boy I despised.

My father steered the horses to the edge of the road and set the hand brake.

I climbed down, a bit unsteady, and waited to regain my land legs as he joined me.

"Stay here," I told Hunter, who gave me a long look and then settled himself again, watchful, as we walked up to the granite step and knocked on the door.

No one answered.

There was no lock, and we had every right to go in, but my father knocked again.

"I suppose Andy might have gone back home," he said. "After what happened this morning, with the constable."

"Maybe." I reached for the handle. "But whether he's still here or not, I'd like to see what there is to see."

I opened the door slowly, and we both went through it, though my father stepped in front of me and went in first.

The potato house was empty.

Nothing but a pallet beneath a window—empty burlap bags someone had piled one on top of the other to make a thin, scratchy, dusty mattress.

I imagined Andy curled there, waiting for the heat of the day to wane so he could sleep.

I walked over to the bedding.

Nudged it with my toe.

Felt something.

Tucked beneath the edge of it: a rubber ball. Red. Chunks of it missing. Something a boy might throw for a dog to fetch.

And I thought again of Buster.

If Andy had lost his own dog in April, why would he carry a ball like this one?

I picked it up.

Looked around once more.

Put it back where I'd found it.

The window nearby was open.

I lay down on the burlap.

"Annabelle, what are you doing?" my father said from the doorway. "Get up from there."

But before I did, I lay for a moment, looking through that window, and imagined the sight of the trees in moonlight. The branches stirring in the breeze. The sound of a whip-poor-will calling out its own name, again and again and again.

When my father turned for the door, I stayed where I was for another moment, lost in my thoughts. Trying to understand what had made me lie down on such a lousy bed. Wishing that I hadn't.

I climbed to my feet and brushed myself off. "He's probably back home by now."

My father closed the door behind us. "Better than starving, I suppose."

And I wondered if that were true.

CHAPTER TEN

"Do you feel up to helping your mother with the last of the berries?" my father asked as we made our way home again that afternoon.

"Sure. I'm fine now." And I meant it. I didn't feel sick or weak anymore. Just a bit crooked. And all my senses wide open, including the one to do with animals. Though none of that had anything to do with work. "Of course I'll help her."

We'd already picked and washed and hulled and canned enough berries for our own winter pies, put up a hundred jars of preserves, sold two thousand quarts at the truck market in Sewickley, shared a few flats with our neighbors, and lost quite a few to the birds and snakes and slugs, so there weren't many left.

But being a farmer means picking every last berry, to sell or give or eat, so pick we did.

And since I would be eating those berries and those

pies, that jam—and since we would pay for the shoes on my feet and the coal for the furnace with the money we earned from selling our crops—it made sense that I would help pick them.

"Then I'll drop you at the patch," my father said, the horses speeding up a little as they closed the distance between us and home.

"What is it, Hunter?" I said without thinking as we neared our lane.

My father stared at me. "What do you mean?"

And he was right. Hunter hadn't made a sound. But I could feel him behind us, sharpening up, coming to attention as we rounded a bend in the road.

"I thought— I thought I heard him growl," I stammered, glancing back to see that he was, indeed, on his feet, his face serious, his eyes on something up ahead.

I turned back to see a truck coming toward us.

I knew most of the old, sunburned pickups that traveled our road.

This one I didn't know.

As it rolled slowly toward us, I saw that the man driving it was a stranger, too.

Not Mr. Graf. I now knew his truck and his face, both, which meant he wasn't a stranger anymore but instead the beginning of someone. A first layer, to which I could add another if I ever saw him again.

The man in the truck coming slowly toward us was brand-new to me. Too old for the war but not old yet. All sharp angles, from his eyebrows to his narrow nose to his pointed chin, a faded hat on his head. And unfriendly. I could tell just by looking at him. Maybe even mean. It was right there on his face as he squinted at us, as if we were too bright. Or he, too dark.

I expected Hunter to bristle at how hostile he was.

But the dog surprised me.

As the truck edged up alongside us, I could sense how calm he was. How full of trust.

Likewise, the man himself seemed to soften as he looked at Hunter standing behind me.

But as the truck passed by, I saw that there was a big cage in the flatbed.

Which I could suddenly smell, too. A thick, hot stench of filth and urine and fear.

"Oh, that's awful." I cupped my hands over my nose, Hunter sneezing behind us.

"What is?" my father asked, looking at me sharply.

"You don't smell that?"

"What, the dust?"

I shook my head. "I don't know." I coughed a bit, deeply upset by the smell, the sight of that cage, the way Hunter twitched and fretted, though the truck was now gone.

"I wonder who that was." My father glanced back over his shoulder.

"I don't know," I said again, trying to imagine a reason for that terrible cage.

"I'd never seen him before," my father said at supper that night.

I gave a piece of chicken to James and another to myself. "Me neither."

My mother passed me the butter. "I wonder if that's the man who moved into the old Steuben place," which was a little farm with a ramshackle house, big barn, fields and gardens left to the birds when Mrs. Steuben moved to Elmira to live with her daughter. "Mr. . . . Edelman, I think. Annie Gribble has been spreading the news about him. Apparently, he's very rude. Tells her to hang up and mind her business every time he places a call."

Mrs. Gribble was the nosy woman who ran the switchboard for all the telephone lines in the township. She often listened in, though she denied it. "A word or two," she always said when challenged, her chins quivering indignantly. "At times I hear a word or two before I'm off the line. Only that. And that's all."

"Apparently he has no family," my mother said. "No interest in being neighborly, no intention of joining the church, none of that."

My grandfather said, "Then he'll make a perfect neighbor for the Woodberrys," who lived next to the Steuben place, their own farm even more run-down. Even sadder.

"Skinny man? Face like a hatchet?" Aunt Lily asked as she wedged two pieces of chicken alongside the mountain of mashed potatoes on her plate. When my father nodded, she said, "That does sound like Mr. Edelman. He came into the post office with the Steubens' old mailbox. Plunked it down on the counter and said he'd pick up his mail. Didn't want it delivered. Wanted us to keep it aside for him." She shook her head. "I ask you: Am I supposed to look after every last thing?"

"How long's he been down there?" my father asked.

Aunt Lily thought back. "Since April."

"Which is when Andy's dog went missing," I said slowly.

Henry frowned at that. "You think Mr. Edelman's a dog thief?"

"I don't know. But Andy's dog is gone. And Buster's gone. And there's another dog missing, too." I told my mother and grandma and Aunt Lily about Mr. Graf from Aliquippa and the bull terrier with the white shoulder.

"I know that man, too," Aunt Lily exclaimed. "He was at the post office, putting up a notice about that missing dog, which he calls Zeus. As if there aren't enough good American names to choose from, and none of them to the glory of some heathen god! And he's offering a reward, too. Ten dollars . . . for a *dog*!"

"I'd pay ten dollars to get Buster back," Henry said sadly.

"Which you won't have to do if Mr. Edelman has him," I said. "He did have a cage in the back of his truck."

"What kind of cage?" When the rolls came around to her, Aunt Lily took a second one though she hadn't yet eaten her first.

"A big one. And I'm sure it was for dogs."

My father peered at me. "How do you know that?"

"I could smell them." Which earned me some curious looks and a deep frown from Aunt Lily.

"Who keeps a dog in a cage?" James said.

"I wouldn't mind seeing a cage or two around here," Aunt Lily snapped. "Nothing wrong with a cage to keep dogs in their place."

My grandma shook her head. "Lily, how a person treats an animal says more about him than almost anything else."

"What does it say when this bunch treats a mangy mutt like royalty?" Aunt Lily said, her mouth full, gesturing at me and my brothers with her fork.

"A good animal is worth more than a bad person," I said.

Aunt Lily glared at me across the table. "As if you can make a comparison like that."

To my mother, I said, "Hunter seemed to like Mr. Edelman all right."

At which everyone turned to stare at me again.

"Since when do you know what Hunter thinks?" James said, a drumstick in his hand.

"She would, if anyone would," my grandfather replied. "I've never seen that dog take to anyone else. And to you, Annabelle, only since, well . . . since you got shocked."

I caught my father frowning at me thoughtfully.

"Speaking of bad people, what's this I hear about that Woodberry boy living in our potato house?" Aunt Lily said, and I was glad for the change of subject.

"He slept there for a night or two while he was working out a problem with his parents," my father said, "but I'm sure he's gone back home by now."

"I should certainly hope so." Aunt Lily added more butter to her potatoes, though the war meant we had less than we used to. "Giving a house over to such a brat. It makes no sense."

It was odd, how I suddenly felt a bit kindlier toward Andy when Aunt Lily called him names.

My father sighed. "The potato house isn't exactly a house, Lily."

"Unless you're a potato," James remarked. At the look on her face, he said, "I didn't mean you, Aunt Lily. You're more like a string bean. Except I don't think there's any such thing as a string bean house. But if there were—"

"James." My mother shook her head at him.

I watched all that, heard it, but was distracted by the man in the truck and the boy in the potato house and the dog waiting for me by the porch steps. By how quickly Aunt Lily would cage up all three if she could.

"Have you ever even talked to Andy?" I asked her, and I noticed my father look up from his plate again, listening.

"No need," she said. "I know his kind. And there's nothing he could say to change my mind."

That night, I dreamed about lightning.

But this time, it wasn't a white-hot bolt that reached down to knock me senseless.

This time, it was slower, more gentle, picking me up and turning me around and around until I was dizzy and disoriented, not sure where home was and where it wasn't.

I woke up confused and unsettled, a good part of me still on that hilltop, the storm receding.

And I realized that I'd spent no time at all on the puzzle of who had saved me.

I'd not forgotten the feel of that rough hand on my cheek, but I was no closer to understanding whose it was. Or why someone had saved my life only to leave me there on my own.

CHAPTER ELEVEN

After a morning of planting and hoeing in the hot sun followed by a quick cold lunch, we set out for Dr. Peck's so he could have another look at me, now that some time had passed.

We usually preferred the wagon and were mindful of the need to ration gasoline during the war, but we took the truck, which was much faster, though just as dusty for Henry and me as we sat in the flatbed and watched the road unspool behind us.

James had kicked up a terrible fuss when we'd left him behind, but my father had said, "Someone needs to look after Grandpap and Grandma," and my mother had added, "Although, if you come with us, Dr. Peck might offer to give you a checkup as well," both of which had done the trick.

Hunter had wanted to come, too, but I had kissed his forehead and told him I'd be back soon.

"That dog sure does like you," James said.

"He'd like you, too, if you'd stop trying to tie his ears in a bow," I'd said as I climbed into the truck with Henry, whose purpose was singular: to look for Buster in places he hadn't searched before.

We both watched for him as we drove along, Henry out one side of the truck, I the other, hoping we'd see Buster tied up in a yard.

As we drove past, I paid special attention to the Steuben place, where Mr. Edelman now lived, its old barn set well away from the road, its even older house begging for some fresh paint and a new roof. And there, that truck in the lane, the cage squatting like a spider in the back.

I saw no sign of Buster.

I thought I heard barking in the distance, but riding in the back of the truck was a noisy business and we were past and away before I had time to listen twice.

"Did you hear that?" I asked Henry.

"Hear what?"

But it wouldn't do to plant a seed I couldn't water.

"Nothing." I tucked the thought into my pocket, wondering whether my father would take us to see Mr. Edelman if Buster didn't turn up soon.

Dr. Peck had a look at the bruises on my chest, which had deepened and spread. He asked if we'd figured out who gave them to me (at which we all said no). Listened to my heart. Did all the usual things that doctors do, tapping and peering and probing in all the usual places.

"These will start to fade in just a few more days," he said as he examined the lightning burns on my arm. "Nothing left but a faint mark that will disappear over time." He straightened up. "No infection, no scarring. You're lucky, Annabelle, to be the same girl you always were."

Behind him, shelves of pouches and jars and canisters and bottles held the medicines and tonics that Dr. Peck made in his apothecary, but I didn't think he had a potion for what the lightning had given me. And I didn't want a medicine for that anyway.

So I thought twice before telling him, telling all of them, what I'd been keeping to myself.

"Actually, I'm not the same girl I've always been."

My mother frowned at me. "What do you mean?"

I looked from her to my father to Henry to Dr. Peck, all of them waiting patiently for my answer. They surely thought I was talking about some dizziness. Maybe some ringing in my ears.

"It's something to do with animals," I said. "Especially dogs."

Into the silence that followed, I added, "Or at least one dog. Hunter. But I seem to know things about birds and horses, too."

"*Things?*" my mother said impatiently. "I don't know what that means."

My father, who had seen me with Hunter, said nothing.

"I've been trying to figure out how to explain it." I sighed with frustration. "It sounds like I'm imagining things."

Dr. Peck held up a hand. "Let's not worry about that. Just tell us what you mean."

Henry took a step closer so he was right alongside the examining table.

"I have an idea about what animals are feeling. Like when Hunter didn't like James tying a vine to his tail. That came from his heart."

"An emotion," the doctor said.

"Yes, but other kinds of feelings, too. What I described earlier, how loud and bright everything is. How everything smells so much stronger than usual—that's how Hunter feels."

My mother huffed. "Annabelle, you're the least silly girl I've ever known, but this sounds pretty silly."

"Now, hang on." Dr. Peck peered into my eyes. "I've read quite a bit about the effects of lightning on people who've survived a strike. Like a man who woke up knowing how to do complex mathematics. And another who could suddenly speak Italian. And *another* who could play the piano without a single lesson. And a woman who could tell what people were thinking. So why not this?" He tipped my chin up, felt my neck, looked at me as if I were a unicorn. "What else is different?"

I shrugged. "Nothing else. Just the animals and the smells and such." I turned to my mother. "That horseradish almost knocked me down."

"Well, that's hardly—"

"Touch, too?" Dr. Peck said, his eyes still on me.

I remembered the feel of the burlap bed on my bare arms. Like needles. "Touch, a bit, but especially smell." I closed my eyes and breathed in deeply. "You had a ham sandwich with mustard on rye bread for lunch." I leaned a bit closer. "And sassafras tea."

His eyebrows went up. "I like that for my gout."

He turned to my parents. "Would you mind if I took Annabelle to Pittsburgh, for an examination at Allegheny General?" At the look on my mother's face, he said, "Nothing invasive. We won't cut her open or anything," which clearly startled her even more and gave Henry a jolt, too.

"*Cut her open?*"

"No, Henry, I'm just talking about an examination." He thought about it. "Maybe a test or two."

My father helped me off the table. "Dr. Peck, Annabelle's been through quite a lot. And—" He looked away. "What you're suggesting sounds . . . expensive."

"Oh, there would be no cost to you. In fact, you—Annabelle, really—would be doing us a favor." He smiled. "Almost everyone who gets struck by lightning is badly hurt or dies. Something like this—to be changed but not damaged—is very rare indeed. It's not often we get to spend time with a miracle."

If Aunt Lily had been in the room, she would surely have given us an earful about what was and was not a miracle.

"Well, then, we'll talk about Pittsburgh, Dr. Peck," my father said. "And we'll let you know."

The doctor sighed. "All right, but these things don't always last, John." He looked at me wistfully. "Sometimes they fade away after just a little while. Like those patterns on Annabelle's arm. This business with her senses and the animals: That could go, too. I would surely like a chance to investigate before it's too late. Tomorrow, if possible."

I felt bereft at the idea. "It might go away?"

Dr. Peck nodded. "As quickly as it came."

"We'll let you know about going to Pittsburgh," my mother said, and something in her voice made me think she wouldn't mind a trip to the city.

"Do that. And let me know if anything else happens, Annabelle."

Though what came next had nothing to do with lightning.

CHAPTER TWELVE

"Don't take too long," my father said as he dropped us at the bridge over Wheeler's Run.

"And stay away from the Woodberrys," my mother added. "And Mr. Edelman's place, too."

"We will," I replied, and I meant it, though if we saw Andy I meant to ask him about Buster, which I could do from the road, without ever getting too close.

Henry and I stood on the bridge and watched the truck pull away, a tail of dust wagging along behind it.

The bridge was one of my favorite places. A shady spot where I could stand and stare at the water rippling like old glass beneath me, the birds at their baths, the sunlight painting itself on the surface of the stream.

On that particular day, I loved the bridge more than ever. The water below played an old tune and carried with it an ancient, underground smell like cold stone, even though the day was warm. And every new leaf unfurling from its bud exhaled a fresh, clean breath. So I stood awash in the mix of the very old and the very new.

Henry and I spent a while there, leaning over the rail, watching the water slip endlessly under the bridge, and I pictured it finding a river, the river a sea, the sea a sky, the sky a storm, the storm a creek like this one. Or even a girl like me.

I imagined the people who had been here long before us, at this same spot, above this same creek, trying to make sense of their own lives. And I imagined those who would come long after us to stand where we stood and do the same.

Such thoughts made me feel like a November leaf. As if the breeze might lift me up at any moment and carry me away.

So I thought again of what was here, and what was now, and what we were meant to do about it.

"Come on." I headed away from the bridge. "Let's go look for Buster."

We walked side by side down the long, straight, flat bottom road, the branches of the trees arching high above us, the leaves framing moments of sun that dappled our skin with skittish light, Henry lengthening his stride to match mine.

I imagined that our hearts were matched, too, as we walked. But I was wrong.

"I don't want to talk to Andy," Henry said as we drew closer to the Woodberry farm.

"Well, I don't, either. But I think we should if we see him."

Henry stopped in a puddle of shade. "He scares me, Annabelle. And I don't want to have to fight him."

Which was an odd notion. "Fight him? Who said anything about fighting?"

My brother was nearly as tall as I was, but he still had to look up to meet my eyes. A slow tide of pink washed across his face.

"That's what boys do. In the schoolyard. When there's something to settle." He made a face. "They fight."

"And you don't want to fight."

"I don't. Not over anything small or stupid, anyway. And not because I can't—though I never have—but because I don't want to. Especially if it's his idea."

I understood that, too. How he didn't want to follow Andy's lead.

"But why would there be a fight about any of this? We're just going to talk to him about a dog."

Henry shook his head. "That's the worst part. Most of the time, when a fight's over, no one can even remember what it was about. Or the reason's so small that it makes no sense."

I'd heard soldiers say as much, about the war. How the

fighting seemed to have a life of its own, like a virus that didn't want a cure.

I looked at my brother intently. "If he's there, you can wait on the road while I talk to him. It won't take me but a minute, and then we'll go on."

Henry hesitated. Started to say something but didn't.

I could feel how torn he was.

But I knew that he would have to be the one to mend the split, if it needed mending.

The Woodberrys ran a small dairy farm that naturally had a strong smell of cow about it and otherwise seemed ordinary enough. At least from the road it did, and I'd never been any closer than that.

We found Andy working on a fence near where we walked.

He looked up, saw us, stared for a bit, and then bent again to his work.

I saw his lips move, and I wondered what he'd said.

"I'll be right back," I told Henry, and made my way into and out of the gully that ran alongside the road, and up to the fence that kept the Woodberry cows contained.

When I reached the spot where Andy worked, I waited for him to look up again.

Eventually, he did. "What do you want?"

Up close, I could see that his nose was still swollen and

bruised. From across the space between us, I could smell how hard he'd been working, though his was a clean sweat.

"I want to talk to you about your dog. And Henry's dog, Buster. Both of them are missing." I was surprised by how calm I sounded.

Andy stood up straight. Laid his pliers on the top of a fence post. Pulled off his work gloves. "My dog's long gone. Two months now."

"What does he look like?"

Andy glared at me. "He's an ugly mutt. With one white eye. Don't know why I want him back."

So his dog was not Buster, and Buster was not his dog. I breathed a sigh of relief.

But then I remembered the red rubber ball I'd found in the potato house and realized that Andy had likely carried it for weeks now, though his pup was gone.

I hadn't expected sympathy to be part of what I felt toward Andy, but I suddenly found that it was easier to dislike the idea of him than to dislike the boy himself, now that he was standing right in front of me.

I changed my mind when he pulled his lips back off his teeth and growled, "But my dog is my business, not yours."

"Maybe not." I glanced over my shoulder. Henry watched us steadily from the road. "But Buster—that's my brother's dog—would want us to find him, no matter how long he'd been gone. Two months. Twenty months. He'd still want us to find him. So we will if we can." I looked carefully at Andy's face. "And you know the same things about your dog. I can tell."

He looked away. "I've already searched everywhere I can think of."

"Everywhere?"

"Except right down there." He gestured with his chin. "Next farm down."

I glanced along the road. "The Steuben place?"

"There's a man named Edelman there now. Mean as a snake." Which meant something, coming from Andy Woodberry.

I thought of the man we'd seen in the truck. "Skinny? Pointy chin?"

Andy nodded. "Sounds like him." He glanced that way. "My pa went over and asked him, but Edelman said he didn't know anything about a missing dog, though he has a few of his own, which are shut up in his barn for some reason. They yap all the time."

As if on cue, a dog began to bark in the distance, and I flinched at the sound.

Andy looked at me more closely. "You afraid of dogs?" he said, curious but with plenty of contempt mixed in.

"Not even a little bit," I said staunchly, though I found myself unsettled without knowing why.

Andy watched me for a long moment, as if trying to decide something. Then he said, "My pa don't want me bothering that man, so I don't."

He ran his hand gingerly over the bruises on his face, and I knew why Andy hadn't gone looking for his dog at the Edelman place.

My parents were nothing like his, but I was still nervous about disobeying them, even though Andy's dog was missing, and Buster was missing, and Zeus from Aliquippa was missing, and a strange man who had just moved in down the road kept his dogs hidden away in a barn and had a big cage in the back of his truck.

"What if we could look for your dog and Buster without bothering Mr. Edelman?" I said.

Andy thought about that. "Dogs bark. Happy or mad, they bark. You go near his dogs, they'll bark. And he'll wonder why."

"And if he's not home to hear them?"

Andy looked a bit less angry. "Then come get me. I'd like to see what's in that barn. And I'd like my dog back."

Which startled me: the idea that Andy would go along.

I realized that he and Betty might have had similar conversations when they were plotting their mischief, and I felt a little sick at the thought.

"But nobody's going to get hurt," I said. "And nothing's going to get broken. Or stolen."

Andy made a face. "Can't steal a dog that's already mine."

When he picked up his pliers and turned again to his work, I noticed that his gloves were worn through in places, the seams sprung from heavy work.

And I thought he looked just as worn out. Too tired for someone so young.

"I hear you got struck by lightning in that storm," he said without looking at me.

He sounded unimpressed. Almost bored.

"I did. Just a little bit."

That brought his head up. "How does a person get struck by lightning *just a little bit*?"

"I guess I was far enough away from where it came down. Though Dr. Peck figured it stopped my heart."

Andy paused, watching my face. "So it killed you? *Just a little bit*?"

I couldn't tell if he was making fun of me.

"He thinks so. But someone brought me back."

Andy looked down again, twisting the wire along the fence with his pliers until it tightened up, all the slack wrung out of it. And I thought again about the wire he'd strung across the path through Wolf Hollow. The one that had cut my brother's face.

I wondered how I could ever feel sorry for a boy who had done such a thing.

So I wouldn't, I decided.

"That sounds like a neat trick," he said. "Bringing someone back to life."

"It was a kindness," I replied, my voice hard. "That's what it was."

And I left him to his work.

Henry fell in alongside me when I came back up out of the gully and went on toward the Edelman farm.

"What did he say?"

"Not much," I replied. "But Buster's not his dog, so that's a good thing."

Henry smiled a little. "It is."

I told him what Andy had said, about Mr. Edelman having dogs shut up in his barn. "Andy thought that was odd. I do, too. He said if we can find a way to search the Edelman place without getting caught, he wants to go with us."

Henry's smile faded. "I don't want him around."

"I don't, either," I replied. "So we'll do things on our own and keep an eye out for Andy's dog while we do it."

For the dog's sake, I told myself. Though I wondered if it would be a mistake to return a dog to a boy like Andy.

CHAPTER THIRTEEN

When Henry and I reached the end of the Woodberrys'
land and the beginning of Mr. Edelman's, we paused and
peered around a border of tall sycamores and thick jewel-
weed. "I don't see his truck," I said.

Henry took a long step beyond the trees that hid us.
"Neither do I."

I followed him slowly along the gully at the front edge
of the Edelman farm.

But before we'd gone very far, I stopped.

"Henry," I said.

I don't know if it was his name or the way I said it that
brought him up short.

He turned. Looked at my face.

I pointed into the ditch, where bits of wind-litter had
snagged on the weeds growing there. A strand of tar paper.

A Baby Ruth wrapper. And Buster's collar hanging from a devil's trumpet.

James had fashioned it for him from a blue bandanna, rolled and tied, for when they played cowboys together, and Buster had seemed to like it, so they'd left it on.

Henry climbed down to pull it free. "It's cut."

I watched as he held the bandanna up to his face.

"Henry, there's blood on it."

He turned it, saw the blood. And looked at me in a way that said quite clearly what I already knew.

"We'll go on in, then," I said. "We'll go on in and find him."

Henry put the bandanna in his pocket, and we walked together along the road until we reached the lane into Mr. Edelman's place.

The house that sat mostly hidden from the road in a grove of trees and wild vines was old and faded. A few slate tiles were missing from the roof. The windows needed washing. The front porch sagged a little. But there were two rocking chairs on that porch, a pot of red geraniums on each step leading up to it, and a bird's nest tucked into a cranny above the steps, the floor beneath it splattered with droppings.

Someone might have easily knocked that nest down, to save themselves the mess and bother.

Someone hadn't.

I wondered about that. And those two rocking chairs. Those flowers, so red and fresh against the old wood of the place. And about Mr. Edelman himself. Whether there might be more to him, too, than met the eye.

From the barn, one of the dogs began to bark. Then another.

Henry glanced over his shoulder. "Maybe we should go get Andy after all."

But I barely heard him.

Every particle of me was focused on that barn. That barking.

"No," I said slowly. "We don't need him."

When I started along the lane toward the barn, Henry followed me, more dogs barking, and harder now, the air hotter than it had been moments before, my heart like a mallet driving a peg into my chest.

The dogs sounded like our church choir at Christmas: loud, earnest, and a little off-key. But mostly I heard how much hurt was in that barn, though it was nicely tucked into the cool shade of a dozen century oaks, its doors open for light and air.

Perhaps it wasn't the oven full of hay dust and yellow jackets I'd imagined, the dogs inside punished in the heat. Perhaps it was a kinder place than that, despite how sad I felt as we came to a stop just outside.

"You really think Buster's in there?" Henry said.

I nodded. "I know he is. I can hear him."

Henry turned to stare at me now, and whatever he saw in my face decided things for him.

"Wait here and keep watch," he said, heading for the door.

But the idea of finding Buster was stronger than my fear of getting caught. So I followed.

The barn was full of shadows, but I could still see that there were pens along the walls of the threshing floor, a dog in every pen.

The smell of the place was strong, a combination of waste and worry that stopped me in my tracks.

"What's wrong?" Henry asked.

But there was no good answer to that.

In the nearest pen was a hound with a white cast on his leg and a long cut down one side of his face, stitched up with black thread, like a torn sleeve. He reminded me of an old man with a cane as he clumped toward us, his bark a little grumpy.

I reached my hand over the gate. When I offered my palm, the dog laid his muzzle in it and sighed.

"Someone broke his leg," I said.

"I can see that," Henry said.

"I didn't say he broke his leg. I said someone broke it."

The difference was considerable.

The beagle in the next pen had three good legs, but the fourth stopped halfway down at a knob of bandage. Her bay was desperate, as if no one had ever listened to her properly.

We watched how hard she tried to stand steady on just three legs, an empty space beneath where her fourth had been.

Another pen held a big dog with a quick, loud bark and some obvious collie in him, all shaved around the middle, with a cinch of white bandage tied in a bow, as if he were a gift.

Henry said, "What happened to him?"

"I don't know. But I can tell that it hurts him to bark."

Though bark he did, as if his life depended on it.

"It's all right, boy," I said. "Everything will be all right."

Each pen had a dish for food, another for water, and a bed of fresh straw. And all three dogs seemed to be recovering from what ailed them.

The last pen was different. It was set apart from the others, with higher fencing around it.

In it stood a big mud-colored bull terrier with a clot of white on his left shoulder, like someone had thrown paint at him, and scabby black cuts all over his face and neck. Every inch of him was muscle and bone. Even from where I stood, I could hear the rumble in his throat.

"That dog's just like the one Mr. Graf is missing." I walked closer. "Same color. Same breed. Same white splotch. But Mr. Graf didn't say anything about him being all beat up like that." I peered through the fence. "I wonder what happened to him."

"And what he's doing here."

"Hey," I said softly, reaching through the fencing, knuckles first. "It's all right, boy. It's okay. We're not going to hurt you."

At first, the dog stayed where he was, his hackles up, head low, but then he came slowly toward me, no wag in his tail, and I felt my own hackles rise.

I quickly pulled my hand back through the fencing.

"This one doesn't seem too friendly. Also like Mr. Graf's dog." I stepped away.

Which was when we heard another dog barking, somewhere past the threshing floor, behind a door I hadn't noticed.

CHAPTER FOURTEEN

On the other side of the door, we found a feed room, empty except for some bales of hay stacked in a pyramid, a long table covered with gleaming tools laid out on a white cloth, and another one covered with a horse blanket—on which my brother's dog lay waiting.

"Buster!" Henry cried.

We ran to his side, Henry murmuring a stream of things a boy might say to a dog he loves, Buster crooning his replies.

I could see how happy Buster was, but I could feel it, too, wrapped up in the smell of his boy: a mixture of soap and dirt, crushed grass, the milk and meat he'd had for breakfast, the brine of his tears, the warm tide of his breath.

But Buster was hurt, too. I could feel that as clearly as I could see it.

Someone had bandaged his left hind leg and one of his forepaws.

"What's wrong, boy?" Henry said.

Buster's answer was an awful attempt to gain his feet.

When Henry began to lift him up, a young woman suddenly burst out from behind the bales of hay and said, "Don't do that! You'll hurt him!"

Henry and I went still.

For a long moment, we stood and looked at the woman. She looked at us. No one said a word.

I reckoned she was maybe twenty or so. Needle thin, in trousers and a man's shirt that was too big for her. She had long yellow hair tied back away from her face. And the palest eyes I'd ever seen.

As I looked at her, I wished I were a painter. Though I would have had to be a good one indeed to capture the look in her eyes. Hard and sweet at the same time. But angry, too. And scared, though I couldn't imagine what was scary about me or Henry.

"Hello," I said.

Nothing.

"I'm Annabelle. And this is my brother Henry. And this is Buster, Henry's dog."

More silence.

"We've been looking for him everywhere."

At which she finally blinked and said, "Who gave you permission to come in here?"

Henry said, "He did," as Buster tried to rise again.

"Lie still!" she cried, rushing forward to hold Buster down, one hand on his flank, the other on his shoulder.

"What's wrong with him?" Henry said, his voice breaking.

"He ran out into the road. In that big storm we had. And my father hit him with his truck."

I imagined Buster waiting at the top of the lane for Henry to come home from Ambridge, trying to escape the terrible noise and commotion when the storm came barging through, running into the road.

"Is he all right?" Henry said. "Will he be all right?"

The woman waggled her head. "I believe so. He seems to be improving just a little."

Buster calmed down as she pulled the blanket up over him.

I said, "His back hurts. And he can't move his hind legs. And he's afraid, though he likes you."

She squinted at me suspiciously. "How do you know that?"

I looked at Buster. Looked back at her. "I just do."

She raised one eyebrow. "You can understand dogs?"

"A bit."

She frowned. "I've been around dogs my whole life, and I can't do that."

"Annabelle was struck by lightning in that big storm," Henry said. "And she's different now."

That startled her. She leaned closer and looked me over carefully.

And then she seemed to make up her mind about us, which smoothed her face out like a warm iron.

"I'm Nora Edelman." She held out her hand.

I was amazed and quite pleased that she hadn't asked any questions about the lightning or what it had done to me.

I took her hand.

Her skin was much tougher than I expected it to be.

I remembered the feel of the hand on my cheek after I'd been struck. The one that had pounded on my chest and brought me back to life.

I couldn't tell if they were the same kind of rough.

She shook Henry's hand, too, and I felt as if we had taken a step toward knowing her.

But then she scrubbed her palm on her trouser leg, and we took a step back toward strangers.

"It was nice of you to look after him," I said, "but we've been worried."

Miss Edelman huffed. "Unlike you, I don't speak dog. How was I to know where he lived?"

Henry gave her a hard look. "Where was Buster when he got hurt?"

She rubbed her nose. "On the road by that farm with all the orchards."

"The McBride farm. And I'm Henry McBride. You might have come to ask about him."

Miss Edelman sighed. "My father and I keep to ourselves. Even so, he did want to do that. Yesterday, when Buster looked to be improving. But I wanted to wait until he was well enough to be moved, so we could take him along, so I could see what his people thought about looking after an injured dog."

Henry gestured back toward the threshing room. "And those other dogs?"

"What about them?"

"Where did they come from?"

She made a face. "I don't know that they're any of your business."

"If you'd brought Buster home to me, we wouldn't be here," Henry said, polite but firm. "But we're here now, and we've every right to ask about a bunch of banged-up dogs hidden in your barn."

Miss Edelman chewed on her lip. "I like gumption, but I don't much like being schooled, especially by a kid." She blew some air out her nose, as if she were a horse. "We help dogs if they need help. Simple as that."

"But you didn't hit all of them with your truck," I said.

"No, but there are other ways to hurt a dog. People set fox traps, but they catch whatever comes along, including dogs like that beagle out there. So we go looking, mostly at night, mostly near water. And if we find animals in traps, we set them free. Or bring home any that are badly hurt."

"Even the wild ones?" I hadn't seen any foxes or raccoons in those pens.

She shook her head. "We turn them loose if they're well enough. If not, we kill them quick and bury them right."

I tried not to picture that. "Those other dogs didn't come from traps."

"No. No, they didn't." She looked at us dubiously. "Mostly we pick up strays. Dogs no one wants. And, I admit, sometimes we rescue one that needs rescuing." She tipped her head toward the threshing floor. "That collie mix out there? We saw him chained in a yard, in the mud, day after day, no shade in the heat, no shelter in the rain. So we took him." There was a fair amount of pride in her voice. Certainly no apology. "He had a broken rib. Like someone had kicked him."

"What about that bull terrier?" I said. "What happened to him?" I gave Henry a look that told him to keep quiet. To see if her story matched Mr. Graf's.

"My father found him by the side of the road to Aliquippa, his leash caught in some thorn bushes. No tags.

Just all those cuts on his face. And a terrible temper." She glanced toward the threshing room. "He didn't like being put in a cage, but he's settled down a lot since he got here."

"I met his owner," I said. "At least I think I did. A Mr. Graf. From Aliquippa, so that part fits. And he described his dog—Zeus, he calls him—as a brown bull terrier with a white patch on his shoulder. And not very friendly. So all that fits, too. Mr. Graf gave my teacher, Mrs. Taylor, his telephone number. In case we saw Zeus."

Miss Edelman listened to all that with a serious face. "Sounds like his dog. Except, well, I don't think Zeus is anyone's *pet*. I've seen wounds like his before. And I believe he got them from fighting. So I'm not inclined to send him back."

I said, "You mean Mr. Graf has other dogs and they don't get along?"

But before she could reply, Henry said, "Maybe Zeus was in a fight after he got loose, nothing to do with where he's from."

"Then why did he run off in the first place?" she said, one eyebrow higher than the other.

"A dog will wander," Henry replied, as if he were my grandpap's echo. "And sometimes get lost." He ran his hand down Buster's back over and over again.

Miss Edelman shook her head. "Dogs know their way home."

"But he was caught in those bushes, or he might have gone back home on his own," I said. "Besides, Mr. Graf seemed like a nice man. He was worried about his dog. And—"

"What someone seems to be and what he really is are often two different things," Miss Edelman said.

"Not always," I said, though I knew she was right.

"No, not always," she said sharply. "But that bull has been through the wringer, and I'm not about to let him go until I know why. And not before I find out something more about your Mr. Graf." She paused. "But if you're right about him, I'll send Zeus home. Fair enough?"

I nodded. "Fair enough. We won't say anything. And you're the one who deserves the reward anyway."

"Reward? What reward?"

"Ten dollars," Henry said. "You could buy a lot of dog food and bandages with ten dollars."

"Or I could keep Zeus right here, where he's safe and has nothing to do but get well." Miss Edelman heaved a sigh. "A reward? People will be searching for him." She gave us a worried look.

"We said we wouldn't tell, and we won't," I insisted.

"Not even for ten dollars?"

I decided not to be angry about that. Miss Edelman didn't know us yet.

"Not even for ten dollars." I thought about the collie

mix with the sore ribs. The old hound with his crooked walk. The poor, sweet beagle. "What do you do with the dogs when they're well again?"

"Find good homes for them. Farms, mostly. Far enough away so whoever had them last won't run into them ever again."

"But you won't give Zeus away?" I said.

"No. I won't give him away." She took one of Buster's paws in her hand and held it gently. "If it were up to me, we'd keep them all, but my father's not particularly fond of dogs."

Which surprised me. "Then why does he do all this?"

She smiled for the first time, and I realized that she was beautiful. "Because he's particularly fond of *me*."

CHAPTER FIFTEEN

I asked Miss Edelman if she'd found a dog with one white eye.

"Well, no, though I know that dog. He came to look at us right after we moved here, my father and I. But he was a healthy dog, not hurt at all, not a stray, just skittish, and after a little visit . . . off he went. Haven't seen him since."

"He's been missing for two months now, since just about when you came here. From the farm right alongside yours, other side of those sycamores. From a boy named Andy, who would like him back." I could hear a little suspicion in my voice.

"Yes. The boy's father came looking." She glared at me. "You think we took that dog away? Gave him to someone in Ohio, maybe?"

I shrugged. "Would you tell me if you had?"

She nodded decisively. "Indeed, I would. No shame in doing what's right, which is what we do, my father and I."

I gave her a long look. "And what would you have done with Buster if we hadn't come here today?"

That knocked her back a step.

Even if she'd been a liar, she might have been disinclined to lie to a girl who could understand dogs. Surely such a girl could smell a fib from a mile away.

And I wished I could. I wished I could do that very thing.

In any case, she told the truth: "I can't say. I don't know." She watched as Buster licked Henry's hand. "When my father first brought him home, I thought we should put this dog out of his misery. He was in that much pain, and it didn't seem likely that he'd walk again. Now?" She shrugged. "Like I said, if you hadn't come along, we would have looked for who'd lost him. But we'd have kept him, if it came to that. Or given him away, though who would want a broken dog if they didn't love him already?"

Henry nodded. "Well, now you don't need to decide. Now I'll take him home."

But Miss Edelman shook her head. "Not yet. Not while he's still healing. And not when a trip over a bumpy road might do him more harm." She pursed her lips. "I've seen two dogs like your Buster, with his kind of injury. One wasted away. The other walked again, though it took some time, and he was never again as nimble as he'd been. So we'll keep Buster here and take care of him and see which road he takes: the downhill road or the one that goes up."

I could see that Henry didn't much like this plan—or being told instead of asked—but in this case, smart was bigger than love, so he said okay. "But I'll help. Every day, I'll come help you with Buster. And with the other dogs, too."

Miss Edelman smiled a little, though it seemed to take an effort. And then she grew serious again. "I don't much like other people coming here. Maybe you, Henry. We'll see. But you mustn't tell anyone about me. Not a soul. Certainly not that Mr. Graf." She looked at each of us in turn. "Do you promise?"

After a moment, Henry asked, "Are you a fugitive from justice?" Which sounded a little silly, like something he might have heard on *Dick Tracy*, but it matched the situation, which was odd and grave.

"I am not," she replied, without a trace of a smile. "I told you before: my father and I—though mostly *I*—are not particularly fond of people, though you two seem more or less tolerable."

Which I took to be a compliment of sorts, though it didn't much sound like one.

"And I'm especially concerned about nasty people,"

she added. "Like the one who hurt that collie out there. I don't want to have anything to do with them. Do you understand?"

"Of course, but there are a lot of nice people around here, too," I said. "You'd like my mother. And my father, who—"

"Well, of course you think your own family is nice," she snapped.

"No," Henry said. "My aunt Lily can be nasty as a barn rat. But our brother, James, is a good boy. And our grandpap is as slow and quiet as a mole, and our grandma's not terribly well, but she's the kindest person I've ever known. Isn't she, Annabelle?"

"She is. But Miss Edelman isn't interested in people in general."

She nodded. "Just what I said. To a T. I'm interested in animals. Dogs especially. And my father's interested in plants."

I thought about the fields beyond the barn, quickly becoming meadows again. "He's a farmer?"

She waggled her head. "Not exactly. He's a geneticist."

At the look on my face, she said, "He's a scientist. He breeds better plants."

And I remembered how my grandpap would sometimes cut down a good, strong sapling so just the stump of it remained and then quickly split that stump to make a cleft and wedge in a peeled shoot off his finest apple tree. And then he'd bind the joint up tight with beeswax so the apple tree would grow quickly from borrowed roots. "A graft won't always work," he had told me, "but when it does, it's quicker and better than planting seeds and a lot cheaper than buying a whole young apple tree."

I looked at Miss Edelman. "Does your father graft trees onto each other?"

She raised her brows. "Sometimes. But what he does is usually more complicated than that. It has to do with using pollen from different plants to create seeds that will produce better varieties."

"Like flowers?"

She shook her head. "Like corn. Wheat. Beans."

I found it interesting that the Edelmans had built their lives around other species. Beans. Dogs.

Though I reckoned the same could be said of farmers like us.

"So do you promise?" she said.

I frowned. "To do what?"

She glared at me impatiently. "What I said before."

I thought it odd to have us promise to keep a secret after she'd already told it.

But I liked that she'd asked us. That the decision was ours.

"We won't lie about everything. We'll have to explain

about Buster and where we found him and why we left him here instead of taking him home."

She didn't like that, but she had been the one to insist that Buster stay with her until he was well enough to travel. So, in the end, she agreed.

"It's no secret that my father lives here, but leave me and the other dogs out of it."

We said we would.

"I mean it, Annabelle. A couple of those dogs came from terrible places, and it would be awful if anyone tried to take them back."

Henry nodded solemnly. "We won't say a word, Miss Edelman."

She spent a moment looking at us. "And don't call me Miss Edelman. Call me Nora or nothing at all."

Henry didn't like to leave without Buster, and Buster clearly didn't like to be left, but off we went anyway, down the lane and away toward home, both of us quiet, both of us different than we'd been an hour earlier as we'd stood on the bridge over Wheeler's Run, contemplating the world as we'd known it then.

I thought about how that world had changed for having Nora in it, though she'd been in it before I knew about her. But now she was in *my* world. And everything was different all over again.

CHAPTER SIXTEEN

"You could really tell what Buster was feeling?" Henry asked as we walked along the cornfields where the bottomland was as flat as an open hand . . . and where I could suddenly hear the corn creaking and popping as it grew, something I'd heard once or twice in the night but never by day.

In the fall, when the corn had been sheared down to stubble, vast flocks of blackbirds would come here to swoop and roil like the shadow of the wind. But for now, the world was green and blue and gold, the young corn snapping and rustling as it grew toward the sky, and I found it almost impossible to believe in the gray to come.

"Annabelle?" Henry said, pulling me back to the here and now.

"Like I said at Dr. Peck's, there were no words. Just . . . notions. Same as Hunter. Same as those other dogs. Though I wish I knew if Buster could understand me, too."

Henry glanced at me in surprise. "He always could, Annabelle. All dogs can."

And I knew what he was saying. That dogs didn't need words.

We walked along, intent on our own thoughts, until mine were interrupted by a cow lowing from somewhere in Wolf Hollow, where cows weren't meant to be. She sounded bereft and lonesome. And I wondered why. And what she was doing there.

But then the sound stopped, and only the idea of her remained. How sad she had seemed.

"Do you remember how that beagle was baying when we went into the Edelmans' barn?" I said slowly.

"Of course I do." Henry thought back. "Like she was scared. And sad."

I nodded. "Which you knew without being struck by lightning."

"Well, you would have, too, Annabelle. You would have anyway."

Maybe. But it was getting harder and harder to know what was really *me* and what was me because of the lightning.

"Do you think Nora was scared of us, when we first got there?" Henry asked.

"I don't know," I replied, distracted. "But I think maybe she was."

Which we'd both sensed without anyone spelling it out.

"I suppose it was having strangers in her barn," Henry said.

"But she wiped her hand after we shook it. Like we were dirty."

He nodded. "I saw that, too. Though I don't think it had anything to do with us, exactly. I think it had to do with us being people."

Most people wiped their hands after petting dogs. Nora, after shaking hands with us.

Something else to ponder as we walked.

After a bit, Henry said, "It makes sense, you know."

I turned to him. "What does?"

"That you can understand animals."

"Why does that make sense?"

He gave me a curious look. "Don't you remember the pigs?"

Which was an odd thing to ask.

"I remember a lot of pigs, Henry." Though we hadn't kept any for a while now.

"You were nine, I think, and I was six or seven. The pigs got out one night, and you and Daddy and I went after them before they could get too far away. You don't remember that night?"

Well, of course I remembered running around in the

dark with Henry and my father, trying to find the pigs, trying to herd them back to their pen, though it seemed an impossible task.

Pigs are fast and slippery and stubborn and contrary. Not easily wrangled.

"I remember how tired we were," I said, "and how dark it was, and how the pigs were roaming farther and farther into the woods."

"And you stopped and suddenly started calling them like they were piggies in a storybook."

I remembered that, too. Calling, "Here, piggy piggy piggy," in a silly, squeaky, whispery voice that must have come from someone I'd imagined myself to be.

"And they came. Do you remember?"

I did. I remembered how they had come out of the darkness, one by one, to follow the sound of my call, until they were all safely rounded up, every last one of them.

I looked at him. "You think the lightning woke up something I already had?"

He shrugged at that. "It had to come from somewhere."

I thought about butterflies and birds. How they knew things they'd never learned—when to fly north, when south—because of knowledge passed down across the centuries, triggered by the slant of the sun, the evening chill.

Maybe, like them, we all knew things we didn't know we knew.

Maybe all we needed was something to wake that knowledge.

Though I reckoned some things were better left sleeping.

And I thought of Andy again. What had woken up in him when Betty came to Wolf Hollow.

When we got home, we found my father and my grandpap with James in the barn, shelling dried corn. James fed the cobs from last season into the sheller as my grandpap turned the crank. And, all the while, my father lugged in more corn and hauled out the full buckets of kernels, ready to crack for the chickens.

The dusty sweetness of the dried corn was so strong that I stopped to bend over, sneezing into my hands, and was newly aware of the stale, musky odor of mouse, old straw, and a century of cow dirt, horse dirt, and the grease that kept the farm machines from rusting.

"We found Buster," Henry said.

My grandpap stopped cranking the sheller.

All was quiet but for the rock doves in the rafters and the thready whistle of wind coming through the boards, as if the barn had lost a tooth.

"Where is he, then?" James looked around.

"He's hurt," Henry said. "And he can't come home until he's well."

Which triggered a flurry of questions from everyone, including my grandpap, who normally listened more than he spoke.

"That man we saw on the road," I said to my father, "Mr. Edelman . . . he hit Buster with his truck during the storm, and he didn't know Buster was ours, so he took him home. And he's been looking after him ever since."

It was clear that my father had several things to say, but he started with "I thought we told you to stay away from Mr. Edelman."

"I know. But we heard dogs barking, and Mr. Edelman wasn't home. So we decided to have a look."

My father squinted at me. "If Mr. Edelman wasn't home, how did he tell you he'd hit Buster with his truck?"

That stopped me in my tracks. "He came home while we were in the barn with Buster," I said, sorry for the lie, wishing I hadn't started down this path.

Lies had been at the root of every big mistake I'd ever made, and here I was lying again. But I didn't know how to keep my promise to Nora otherwise.

"Daddy, we *had* to go into that barn," Henry said. "Annabelle knew Buster was in there, didn't you, Annabelle?"

My grandpap frowned at that. "You knew him by his bark?"

I turned to my father. "Didn't you tell them? About what I said at Dr. Peck's?"

But my father shook his head. "I figured it was your story to tell."

James and my grandpap looked at me intently, waiting for an explanation.

"Okay." I measured the afternoon by the shadows that slanted in through the high windows of the barn. "But let's wait for when Grandma and Aunt Lily can hear it, too. So I can tell it just once."

James groused about that, curious as a cat, but I wouldn't be rushed. "I'll go in and help Mother get supper. It won't be long."

"Give me a hand with these pails first." My father handed me a bucket full of corn, picked up two himself, and headed for the feed room.

I followed him to where we stored the grain, safe from every kind of critter except the mice, which took only a little for themselves.

"I talked to Andy," I said as I emptied my pail into a big bin. "He was out near the road as we went by."

My father paused. He looked like he had something to say, but he waited.

"I asked if he'd seen Buster." I poured away the last of my corn and stepped out of the dust that rose from the bin.

My father emptied his, too.

We both waited for the air to clear, the barn creaking a bit, like an old man rising from a chair.

I handed him my empty pail. "What you said—about how I reminded Andy of bad things. It bothered me. So I thought I'd see if that was true."

My father stacked the pails. "And?"

I shrugged. "I think he's angry about everything, not just me."

"Like his parents?"

"Do you mean like his parents are angry? Or like Andy's angry about them?"

"Both, I suppose. And how his dog ran off. How hard he has to work all the time, I guess." He paused. "Lots to be angry about."

But I had known Andy for a long time. Long enough to remember him as a little boy.

He'd been devilish, yes. But not so angry. Not so mean.

And not nearly as weary as he seemed to be now.

"What you told us at Dr. Peck's," my father said, choosing his words. "About how you can understand animals."

I waited. "You don't believe me?"

"Oh, I do, Annabelle. I don't understand it, but I believe it." He smacked some yellow corn dust from his sleeve. "I'm just curious about whether you can do that because you already had a knack for understanding *people*."

"You think I'm good at understanding people?"

He shrugged. "You understood Toby better than anyone, though he didn't make it easy."

"I guess I did." He wasn't wrong about that.

"And Betty."

But that wasn't true. "I didn't understand *her*, Daddy. Not at all."

He gave me an apologetic look. "No, I didn't mean it like that. Just that you saw quite clearly what she was."

"But only because she showed me."

He nodded. "And she showed something quite different to the rest of us."

"What does this have to do with Andy?" I said.

He sighed. "I'm not sure it does. But someone who understands people and animals well would know the answer to that, if anyone would."

As I stood there with my father, I remembered something lost in the tumble and blur of everything that had come since. A spring day at the schoolhouse when I was perhaps seven. Andy perhaps nine. At recess, we'd found the nest of a house sparrow fallen from its nook. Four hatchlings dragging themselves through the grass, their mother hovering above them, frantic. Helpless. Alarmed by us children who must have seemed like reckless giants as we darted among her stranded babies.

Until Andy picked up the nest, wedged it back in its nook, and then used a pair of oak leaves so as not to leave his scent on the scrawny chicks as he scooped them up and tipped them back where they belonged.

One of them had been injured when it fell. I remembered its crooked wing. How hard it had tried to nestle among the others. How impatient they had seemed.

I'd thought of those baby birds all through the hours that followed—dreamed of them that night—and followed the idea of them down the path through Wolf Hollow the next day.

But when I arrived at the schoolhouse, I'd found Andy digging a hole, the broken bird dead on the ground, its eyes pecked out, ants boiling from their sockets.

"It's the law of nature," Mrs. Taylor said as we watched Andy fill in the hole. "Survival of the fittest."

At the time, I'd been sure that I'd never forget the look on Andy's face.

And yet I had.

CHAPTER SEVENTEEN

When my father went back toward the threshing floor, I headed off to help my mother get supper ready, my feet finding their way as I thought about what my father had said. About Andy. About me.

And I spent more time with those hatchlings. The ones who had survived. The one who hadn't. The only difference being their angle of descent: how one had fallen harder than the others, landed wrong, through no fault of its own.

It scared me, how so much depended on small things. On chance. On things beyond my control.

But I told myself that there were plenty of things I *could* control, too. Plenty of things I myself could decide.

Just like Andy could. Just like anyone could.

"There you are," my mother said when I stopped in the mudroom to shed my boots.

It was a relief to see her there at the kitchen sink, right where I expected her to be.

I didn't mind going in to help with supper each day while my brothers stayed outside doing chores until I rang the front-porch bell that called them to supper from however far away they might be.

On those summer afternoons, my mother and I had the house to ourselves, the breeze filling the thin white curtains while birdsong from the garden blended with the sounds we made chopping vegetables, stirring whatever simmered in the pots on the big cast-iron stove, the clatter of cupboard doors and footsteps, our voices as we talked about the day.

On this day, we spoke of things that might be waiting for something to wake them up.

"Will you tell me about your grandparents?" I said as I peeled potatoes and quartered them for the pot. They were from last year's crop, and they had brought with them from the root cellar the distinctive scent of earth steeped in decades of beets and carrots, turnips and radishes that wept and wilted throughout the long winter months.

"My grandparents?" My mother was grating cabbage for slaw, and the wet sweep of it against tin teeth, over and over again, was summer in one sound.

"Did they do anything . . . unusual?"

My mother stopped, the wedge of cabbage poised in her hand. "You mean like talk to dogs?"

I bowed my head. "Are you making fun of me?"

My mother went still. "I'm sorry, Annabelle. I didn't mean it to sound like that. I just don't know what to think about all this."

"Me neither. But I'm trying to understand it. And I wonder if it comes from something that was always there, deep down."

"Inherited, you mean? Like brown eyes?"

I nodded. "I suppose. Daddy thinks it comes from my understanding people well, but anyone can do that if they try hard enough. So I reckoned there must be something more to it."

My mother gave me a dubious look. But then she put the cabbage on the cutting board, laid down the grater, wiped her hands on her apron, and went into the front room. I heard her open the cupboard.

The sound of her shoes as she came back was all brisk business, but the light in her eyes was something else altogether as she set down our big album of photographs on the kitchen table and began to turn the pages of thick paperboard. Each one was adorned with a dusty brown photograph framed in an oval window and a name written in pale blue ink underneath.

From time to time she would gather us together at the kitchen table and tell stories about the people on those pages, as if we were in a school that taught us memories not our own, though I felt as if I, too, remembered those people from long ago. As if a shared bloodline was also a shared storyline. As if we were like those butterflies and birds, born with the knowledge of others who had come before them. How to navigate by stars. Where to go when the wind blew cold.

Here, at our kitchen table, my mother triggered what was mine.

"There." She tapped a picture of a man and a woman in wedding clothes. The woman held a bouquet of drowsy flowers. On her head, a crown of ivy. The man wore a dark jacket long enough to cover his knees. Neither one of them was smiling.

The woman looked a lot like my mother. Maybe even a little like me. I already knew who she was. "My great-grandmother. Your grandmother."

I heard my mother swallow. "Blanche." She paused, her finger gentle the page. "She was to *me* what Grandma is to *you*." She swallowed again.

I waited. It was not often that my mother stopped what she was doing to go slowly and quietly into her memories.

"I've told you what she was like when she was my grandma. But when she was a girl, she lived in Pittsburgh. In a house with gaslights and windows ten feet tall. And a piano." She stroked the portrait with the tip of her finger.

"She left that house long before I was born, but she took the piano with her. Played it every single day for as long as she lived. Even on the days when her children were born." She smiled at me. "Especially on those days."

I imagined that. I imagined fingers like my mother's, strong as anything. "What happened to the piano?"

My mother straightened up. She closed the book carefully and wiped her face with her hands. "When she died, my grandfather took it into the graveyard where they buried her. And he burned it."

I couldn't think of a single thing to say about that, but I knew I would remember it for the rest of my life.

"For years after that, when we went to visit her grave, I found the blackened keys still scattered in the grass, and even the metal strings, coiled among the ivy along the edge of the graveyard."

"What did she like to play?"

My mother smiled. "Everything. Songs and classical pieces, lullabies, music she invented."

I thought about wild geese, like the point of a vast arrow, flying south.

Or the orioles coming home in the spring, singing to each other on fair mornings, their songs as bright and clean as rainwater.

"Did your mother play the piano, too?" I asked.

"As a girl. But when she got married, and had children, and had no piano anymore . . . well." My mother returned to her work.

"And you never played, either?"

My mother didn't turn around. "No, I never did. Though sometimes I thought I'd like to try." She grated the cabbage with sure and rhythmic strokes. "I used to dream that I played," she said. "And I would wake up feeling as if I knew how."

CHAPTER EIGHTEEN

"Mr. Edelman admitted that he hit Buster with his truck?" Aunt Lily said, one eyebrow cocked. "And has been looking after him ever since?"

We were at the table, passing dishes of pork chops crusted with brown fat, potatoes stewed with onions and pepper, a bowl of slaw, and the last of the lima beans canned the year before, freshened in a hot butter bath.

I looked at Henry and he at me. We had promised we wouldn't say anything about Nora or the other hurt dogs. They were her business—and a little bit ours—but no one else's. Not yet.

"He didn't mean to hit Buster," I said, which was surely the truth. "Mr. Edelman isn't as nasty as he seems."

Aunt Lily squinted at me. "He didn't mind you sneaking around his place?"

It was a question I couldn't answer without another lie.

"He didn't say a word about that," Henry said. Which was, in fact, the truth, since he hadn't even been home.

My mother put down her fork. "Your father and I told you not to go near that man."

"I saw Buster's collar in the gully along the road," I said. "It had blood on it. And Mr. Edelman's truck wasn't in the lane. So we decided to have a quick look in the barn, just to see if Buster was there."

My father looked from me to Henry and back again. "You saw blood on his collar, and you didn't think to come get me?"

Henry looked down at his plate for a moment. "We were right there."

"We just wanted a quick look," I said. "And there were red geraniums and rocking chairs and a bird's nest on his front porch."

"Which has nothing to do with anything," Aunt Lily snapped.

Though I saw a different thought cross my mother's face, and I reckoned that the idea of flowers and rockers had let her see Mr. Edelman in a kinder light. As it had for me.

"And Annabelle could hear Buster calling," Henry said.

At which Aunt Lily rolled her eyes. "More nonsense about dogs. One mutt sounds like another, Henry."

"To you, maybe, but not to Annabelle."

My grandpap turned to me. "Is this the story you said you'd tell us at supper?"

"What story?" my grandma asked, her coffee cup poised halfway to her lips.

And everyone looked at me, waiting.

"The one I told Dr. Peck this morning. And he said it wasn't impossible."

"What wasn't?" Aunt Lily said. "Surely not more dog fiddle."

"I suppose it will sound like fiddle to you," I replied. "But the truth is that, well, I can understand dogs now. And other animals, too. *Just a bit*."

For a moment, silence.

Then, "Finally!" James said. "A proper superpower. Did you ask Buster why dogs are always sniffing somebody's butt? Though—"

"James!" Aunt Lily squawked. "That's quite enough of that." But I saw my grandfather hide a smile behind his hand.

"What do you mean, you can understand dogs now?" my grandmother said.

I shook my head. "It's hard to explain."

"And it's hard to believe," Aunt Lily said. "Though it's clear that *you* believe it. Which proves that you're truly garbled from the lightning." She looked around at the others. "You know I'm right. Girls do not speak *dog* unless their brains are scrambled. Am I right, Father?"

My grandfather shrugged. "If you are, then by all means feel free to scramble *my* brains." He smiled at me. "I've met many a dog that surely had more ideas worth hearing than most people I've known."

"You believe me?"

"I do indeed." He noddded. "All this lightning business has shook me up some, I'll not deny it. But having been shook, I feel quite calm about a granddaughter who can talk to dogs."

"Well, anyone can talk *to* dogs," I said. "It's the other way around that's harder."

"Oh, for Pete's sake, you've all gone mad." Aunt Lily helped herself to another chop. "And without lightning for an excuse."

"Annabelle's not mad," Henry said. "She's the smartest kid for miles."

Aunt Lily reached for the potatoes. "A person can be mad and smart at the same time."

James gave her a thoughtful look. "Like a mad scientist."

"It's all nonsense," she said. "Every bit of it."

"But it isn't," Henry said. "And you wouldn't think it was, if you'd been there to see her with Buster."

Aunt Lily huffed at that. "Even if it were true, which it isn't, what does lightning have to do with dogs?"

At which I said what I'd been thinking all day long. "Maybe the lightning unlocked something I already had. Passed down from someone else."

"Does that mean somebody in our family was a dog?" James asked. He was quite serious, which made it all even funnier. But no one laughed, though my grandfather's shoulders shook a little, and Aunt Lily made a *tch*ing sound before she turned back to her plate.

"Not a dog," I said. "But maybe someone who got along well with animals."

My father sighed. "I doubt Dr. Peck will find a better explanation. But I think he was right. About a trip to Pittsburgh."

At which James and Aunt Lily launched a barrage of questions about who would go, and when, and whether James could visit the zoo, Aunt Lily the museum, until my father held up his hand for silence.

He pushed his chair back. "I'll telephone him now to see about going to the hospital."

"And to the zoo?" James said.

My father shrugged. "I don't know what they have that would be any more interesting than what we've got right here."

"Well, we haven't got any baboons," James muttered. "And I'd like to see if Annabelle can speak lion, too."

"Can I talk to him?" I said as my father and Dr. Peck settled on their plan.

My father gave me a look before handing over the receiver.

I held it a bit away from my ear so Henry, at my side, could hear the conversation, too. "Hello, Dr. Peck. . . . Yes, I'm fine, thank you. I just wanted you to know that I will come and let those other doctors have a look at me, but only if they examine my brother's dog, Buster, too."

"Annabelle!" My father reached for the receiver, but I stood fast, listening to what Dr. Peck was saying about dogs not being allowed in hospitals.

"Then I won't go," I said, though I took care to say it politely. "He needs someone to fix his back. Or at least tell us what's wrong with it."

I listened some more. Thanked the doctor. Said goodbye. Turned to my father. "Dr. Peck knows a veterinarian in the city who has an X-ray machine. He's going to arrange an exam for Buster while the doctors at the hospital are examining me. First thing in the morning."

My father rubbed his jaw. "I seem to have rather strong-headed children." Though he didn't sound sorry.

"What about me?" James said from the doorway.

"The strongest," my father replied.

Which made James hop in place, his face candle-bright.

CHAPTER NINETEEN

After supper, after redding up the kitchen, after the boys went out with my father to put the cows and the horses to bed, after my grandma and grandpap settled down to listen to the radio, my mother and I spent the last of the light in a pepper patch where the weeds had had their way for far too long.

"Just aren't enough hours in the day," my mother said as she worked. "Even in June."

But the evening was cooling down, with a breeze skipping over the top of the hills, and I was content with the chore we'd come to do, hoeing up the chickweed and hogweed that grew and grew and refused to be banished, though we did our best.

I thought about that as I worked. About what made something a weed (something to kill) and what made something else a flower or a crop (something to tend).

"What makes something a weed?" I asked my mother.

She paused. "I suppose it depends on where it is. In a garden, it's the plant you can't eat, the one that tries to take over ground meant for what you *can* eat."

"So if chickweed tasted good?"

"I suppose we'd be pulling up the pepper plants instead."

We worked on for a while to the pleasant thunk and scrape of our hoes against the rocky dirt.

"Who's that?" my mother said suddenly, straightening up.

I turned to see a truck coming down the lane toward us.

This was a truck I knew.

And a man I knew driving it.

"That's Mr. Graf. The man I told you about, who lost his dog Zeus."

We waited as he pulled to a stop alongside the pepper patch and climbed out of his truck.

"Hello," he said as he walked toward us, peering at me curiously. "I know you. From the schoolhouse."

"That's right," I said.

The first time I'd seen Mr. Graf, I hadn't yet met Nora or Zeus, and I'd been able to look at him with my eyes alone.

This time, I knew where Zeus was.

I knew a secret I wasn't supposed to tell him.

I knew that Nora had her doubts about him. And that someone had hurt his dog.

But I was reassured by the gleaming smile he gave me. It was such a beautiful smile. And when he took off his hat, I saw that his hair was clean and thick and a deep walnut brown.

As at the schoolhouse, he wore town clothes. Polished boots.

"This is my mother," I said. "Mother, this is Mr. Graf."

"Call me Drake," he said, looking at me first and then at her.

She smiled at him. "I understand you're looking for a lost dog."

"I am. Did your daughter tell you about the reward?"

At which my mother nodded, her smile fading a little. "She did. But that doesn't change anything. We haven't seen your dog, Mr. Graf."

Which wasn't a lie, since she thought it was the truth.

"I've been looking all over." He sighed. "And I've heard about other dogs missing, too. But you don't know anything about that, either?"

"Not a thing," my mother said, and I was relieved that Henry and I hadn't said anything about the dogs in Nora's barn.

"You must really love that Zeus," I said. "To be searching for him so hard."

Mr. Graf nodded. "He's quite a dog."

I remembered the moment when I'd reached into the bull terrier's pen. The look in his eyes. Like he was sizing me up.

"We'll let you know if we see him," my mother said, returning to her work.

But Mr. Graf spent another long moment looking at her until she glanced up and caught him staring.

He tipped his hat. "I hope you will."

And we watched as he returned to his truck and drove farther down our lane to where it was wide enough to make a turn.

When he passed us again, he smiled and waved.

"What an odd man," she said when he was gone.

"What do you mean?"

She leaned on her hoe. "I don't know. There was something about him."

"He seems nice enough," I said.

But then I remembered how kind my mother had been to Toby in his grungy black coat and hat, his long guns hanging down his back, his smile as rare as a November plum.

She had trusted him, though he had been a hard man to know. It had been work, to know him. Confusing sometimes.

In comparison, the clean and tidy Mr. Graf with his perfect smile and fine manners was easy.

"I hope you're right," my mother replied. And there

was something in her voice that made me wonder what I might be missing.

Whether I only saw what people showed me. Which was never all there was to see.

Toby had taught me that. So had Betty.

When twilight put an end to our chores, my mother and I walked tiredly down the lane to the house and found the others gathered around the radio, listening to the war news, my grandma nodding in her chair, my brothers stretched out on the floor in their pajamas.

"That Mr. Graf came by looking for his dog," my mother said as she settled on the couch alongside my father. "I didn't think much of him."

My father glanced at her in surprise. "Did he do something?"

She shrugged. "No. I just thought he was a bit . . . off. But Annabelle didn't, did you?"

I shrugged. "I did wonder if he'd been in the war. When I first met him."

We all knew young men who had gone to war as one thing, come home as something else.

"Well, his dog's not here, so he has no reason to come back." My father settled again, and we all listened to a report about bombs in Romania. The tide of the war turning there. The end in sight but still too far away.

CHAPTER TWENTY

We didn't tell Aunt Lily that Buster would be going to the city with us until we pulled up in front of the Edelman farm.

"We're taking a dog to Pittsburgh?" She sat up straight. "Not in my car we're not."

"Then we'll take the truck instead, and you can stay home," my father said. "It's up to you, Lily."

When she didn't say anything more, Henry and I got out of the car. "We'll be right back."

"I can drive up to the barn, Annabelle."

"No, wait here. We'll be along in a minute."

And before my father could say anything else, Henry and I took off down the lane toward the barn.

Once again, there was no truck in the lane, and I pictured Mr. Edelman roaming around the countryside, looking for strays.

The dogs didn't make too much noise when we ran through the big open door. They knew us now, and they wagged their tails as they made their way to the gates of their pens to greet us.

All but Zeus, the big bull terrier. He stood foursquare with his nose up against his gate and stared at me, his eyes small and round, pale as water.

As I watched, he licked his chops with a long pink tongue.

"What's wrong?" Nora said as she came out of the feed room all at once, wiping her hands on a rag.

"Nothing," I replied.

"Then why are you here at the crack of dawn . . . and why the duds?" She flapped a hand at the dress I wore, my Sunday best.

"We've come to collect Buster. To take him to Pittsburgh for an X-ray. And early was the only time the doctor could see him."

Henry explained everything in a word or two, without any fat on the bones, and she nodded her approval. "Though I don't like to move him," she said doubtfully. "And I'll want to wrap him well so he stays as still as possible."

"Then let's wrap him," Henry said. "The others are waiting in the car, and I don't want them coming to look for us."

"Well, neither do I!" Nora exclaimed. She looked like she'd eaten a lemon. "I was afraid of this. People coming here where they don't belong."

"They won't," I said. "But let's get this done."

Nora led us again into the feed room, where Buster lay whining and whimpering on a bale of hay. I could feel the joy rolling off him in waves, but it was mixed with pain, and the result was wonderful and terrible and strange.

"I'll hold him still," Henry said quietly, but Buster knew what to do, and he did it well, lying without moving as Nora wound a white cloth snugly around his body, through his legs, and down the length of him and then around and around until he was bound securely.

While she worked, I told her about Mr. Graf coming for a second time to look for his lost terrier. "I'm surprised he hasn't come here, too, on his own, like he came to our place."

"He won't get in this barn," Nora said, her voice grim. "I won't have people coming here, Annabelle. You—well, it's too late. You're already here. But if you tell anyone about me and the dogs—"

"I didn't say anything about anything," I insisted. "And I won't. Not unless it's okay with you."

"I won't, either," Henry said.

She paused, looking at us in turn. "I'm counting on you."

Then she made a broad sling out of a horse blanket and passed it carefully under Buster's belly so I could lift from one side and Henry from the other, which was awkward and difficult but necessary.

"You mustn't let him put any weight on his legs," Nora said. "And you mustn't twist him at all. His back has to stay straight."

"All right," I promised, struggling a little, though Buster wasn't a big dog.

And we turned to go, Buster swinging lightly between us.

Once Buster had had his welcome-backs and we were on our way again, I decided I'd look straight ahead, down the road toward Pittsburgh, and wouldn't spend a moment on the Woodberry farm as we passed by. But my eyes seemed to have a mind of their own, turning to see if Andy was there again, as he'd been before, along the fence line.

He wasn't.

"What a mare's nest," Aunt Lily said, staring out at the distant barn, the lousy little house. "Not a thing about it worth the bother."

It was something I myself might have said, but I found it nasty, coming from her.

I thought about that as my father drove toward the city and Aunt Lily told him how to do it, every step of the way, until I was weary of the sound of her voice.

She sat up front with my father, James on the seat between them. My mother sat in the back with Henry and me, Buster laid carefully across our laps.

It wasn't easy to hold still as we made the long drive, but Buster needed stillness, so stillness we gave him.

Even so, I could turn my head at least, and did, from one side to the next, amazed at all the sights as we trundled along the Ohio River toward the city. But when we reached Pittsburgh, I was tempted to close my eyes, and I held my breath for as long as I could, through the yellow fumes of brimstone from the steel mills, past the smokestacks tipped with flames like giant matches, all of it something the devil might have thought up.

To the south, across the greasy brown river, beyond the steel mills, the hills rose up steeply, covered with layers of little houses all blackened with soot, and I imagined standing high above them, looking down on the rows of houses, as if they sat on stairs leading to a dirty cellar, dark and crowded with furnaces and pipes and all the contraptions that everyone wants but no one wants to see.

"How can people stand it here?" I cupped one hand over my nose, the other over Buster's.

My mother sighed. "They don't have much choice. They have to eat."

"But can't they find something better to do? A better place to live?"

She shook her head. "I believe they would if they could. But most of those people came here with nothing. And I do mean nothing, Annabelle."

I thought about my own house and decided that I would never complain about anything ever again, though I knew I would.

"And don't forget," my father said, "that every warplane, every battleship, every tank is made from the steel milled in factories like those. So it's not just the airmen and the sailors and the soldiers who are fighting the war."

I tried to imagine what it would be like to spend long summer days in those huge mills, melting metal and pouring it into molds, so hot that my boots filled up with sweat. So filthy that I had to take off my clothes before I went inside at the end of the day.

When Buster began to whine, Henry took one of his paws. "He must hate this."

My mother said, "He must wonder why we'd ever come to a place like this."

"He does," I said. "He doesn't understand any of it."

CHAPTER TWENTY-ONE

When we got to the city, we dropped Aunt Lily off at the museum first, though she grumbled that it wasn't even open yet. "And what am I to do until then?" she groused.

"You'll be the first one in the door," my father said through the car window. "You'll have the place all to yourself."

"With time to see a smidgen only. Which is absurd. And most unfair." She shook her finger at him. "And don't be late fetching me! When you say noon, I expect to see you at noon and not a minute later."

I wasn't the only one smiling as we pulled away.

Next, the zoo, which was another massive, imposing place, though this one made me think of a prison, no matter how brightly the gardens bloomed.

As James got out of the car, my father said, "Don't climb over any fences."

"I won't," my mother replied, which made James laugh.

"And don't stick your arm through the bars."

"We'll be fine," my mother replied. "And if James misbehaves, I'll trade him in for a monkey."

"Hey!" James yelped, though within moments I heard him say, "I'd make an excellent monkey. Except for the part about eating bugs. Though—"

And then we were away.

I'd been tempted by the zoo and all its exotic inmates, despite the cages. Especially the slow-motion giraffe, swinging its great mast of a neck, its knobby horns, its long black river of tongue. But I'd been there before.

I'd been even more tempted by the museum, a huge, pale building with statues of women in dark robes looking down from the rooftop. I longed for the paintings it held, even if I had to see them with Aunt Lily by my side. But I'd been there before, too.

I saw something different as we made our way toward the animal hospital, none of it grand. But even the grungy blocks of ordinary city made me want to slow down and spend time on them as we drove down one street after another past shops full of things we didn't own, couldn't make for ourselves, didn't need. And row houses everywhere, some of them rather fine with brick facades and striped awnings. Other stumpy and sad, their faces dirty, a few with people on their stoops.

Every block was like a book, every page at first glance the same but surely different if I could just read it, all of it passing too quickly for that.

But as we drove deeper into the city and along a broad street lined with shops and taverns and offices, the traffic slowed and stuttered, giving me time to spend on the details of the place.

I gazed out the open window at the chaos and commotion. The bright, neon language of the signs, like bottled rainbows. The snap and bustle of people rushing like ants along the sidewalk. A streetcar on rails, clanging and clattering as it trundled down the middle of the street, packed full of people in hats and blank faces.

The air was gritty and smelled unclean, like a privy and a butcher shop all at once. And the ground was entirely covered with pavement and grates and tar.

I would have needed a calendar here to tell me that this was June.

But I was still a bit sorry when we finally pulled up in front of the animal hospital, a little building that looked like a shoebox.

When my father got out of the car, Buster lifted his head and whined.

"We're here," Henry told him. "We're here to get you well again."

I could feel what Buster felt as he gazed at my brother: part trust, part hope, part fear, too much pain.

My father came around and gently gathered Buster off our laps, both of his arms under the dog's belly. "Let's get this poor boy inside."

I followed my father and Henry into the animal hospital and up to the counter where a nurse was waiting.

"You must be Mr. McBride," she said, smiling. "And this must be Buster."

I was amazed that, at a place like this, in a city like Pittsburgh, anyone would know us before we'd had a chance to say who we were and why we'd come.

"Dr. Peck made all the arrangements in record time." She looked curiously at Buster. "This must be one special dog."

"He is," Henry said, his voice shaking a little. "I'll be back for you soon, boy." He stroked Buster's soft ears and kissed his head until a nurse came and rolled him away on a gurney, through a set of swinging doors and out of sight.

And then we went to the hospital where other doctors were waiting for me.

This one was a lot bigger than the one for dogs: a huge, tall white stone wedding-cake of a building wedged on the side of a steep hill.

Standing before it, I felt small enough to fit in a vest pocket.

"Do we really have to go in there?" I craned my neck to look up the long, stern face of the hospital.

"Unless you expect the doctors to come out here and examine you on the sidewalk," my father said.

And with that we went cautiously through the hospital doors and into a huge lobby. It smelled like the orange Mercurochrome my mother had painted with a tiny glass wand over every skinned knee or elbow I'd ever had.

My father led the way across the lobby to a big front desk where several people sat talking on telephones and giving directions.

One of them beckoned us forward. "Can I help you?" she said briskly.

"We're here to see Dr. Peck," my father replied, "and some other doctors whose names we don't know."

"Well, let's start with *your* name, shall we?"

"McBride. The, um, patient, is Annabelle. Annabelle McBride."

She nodded. Dialed a number on her telephone, which was shiny and black and sat on the desk. "Annabelle McBride here to see Dr. Robinson."

She listened for a moment and then hung up the phone.

"Neurology. Just down that hall there. Room 108. They're expecting you."

CHAPTER TWENTY-TWO

I knew there would be some things about the day that I would probably forget, but not the sight of Dr. Peck and three other doctors in white, waiting for me, curiosity shining from their eyes.

Nor would I forget the way they peered into my ears and eyes and down my throat, listened to my pulse, tested my reflexes, and finally asked me what had happened during the storm and since.

Nor the way my father said "No," when they asked if they could take samples of my blood, keep me at the hospital for a day or two—for "observation"—and conduct some other, more "intensive" tests to measure my results against those of "healthy girls my age."

"Annabelle *is* healthy," my father said. "So you'll have to be satisfied with what you've got."

His voice held no ire, but I knew he wouldn't budge.

Dr. Peck sighed. "Well, to be honest, most routine tests won't tell us much more than we already know, so we won't waste your time with them. And the ones that might tell us something of interest are too invasive, so I don't blame you for refusing them." He stopped and looked at me thoughtfully. "Can you tell them what it felt like to be struck?"

"Like being stung all over by wasps. Inside and out. Very hot and painful. I'll never forget it."

"No, I don't suppose you will," said Dr. Robinson, who was older than the rest and had a red beard tipped with white, like the tail of a fox.

"And then someone pounded on my chest until I woke up," I added.

Another of the doctors, whose badge read MICHAELS, said, "Someone had good instincts."

Dr. Simpson—the youngest one, with blue eyes and a thin nose—said, "No sign of hypoxia," which, he explained, happened when the body didn't get enough oxygen. "But tell me more about the . . . er, communicating with dogs." There was something in his voice that made me mad.

"You don't believe me?"

The doctor gave me a small smile. "It's not a matter of believing. I trust evidence."

"What you see with your own eyes?"

He squinted a bit. "Yes, I suppose."

I looked straight back at him. "And can you see a fever?"

"No, but I can see the evidence of it. So I know it exists."

The other doctors, my father, Henry, all watched us carefully.

"Well, I'm right in front of you. And I'm telling you the truth."

Dr. Robinson stroked his red beard thoughtfully. "We're not suggesting that you're lying, Annabelle. It's clear that you believe what you're saying. But unless some dog can learn to speak English and verify your claims, there's no way to be sure of anything, one way or another."

"You can come with us to get Buster if you like," Henry said. "And Annabelle can translate for you."

Which made the doctors smile. "Perhaps we can visit you on your farm instead, in a few days," Dr. Robinson said. "By then maybe we'll know the right questions to ask."

"Can you at least tell me why everything is brighter and louder than before?" I asked. "And why everything smells much stronger? And tastes so strong?"

They talked about the possibilities, but in the end it boiled down to "We don't know for sure."

"Some ailments of the central nervous system dull the senses. Take away taste and smell entirely," Dr. Robinson said. "So on the whole I'd say you got the better end of the stick."

I looked from one doctor to the next. "Why did you believe me when I told you that all my senses were on high alert?"

They seemed puzzled by the question. "Why wouldn't we?"

"I didn't give you any proof. No evidence at all."

The youngest doctor nodded, smiling a little. "I see your point. But I suppose that's easier to accept because we have the same senses you have. If yours are sharper right now, that doesn't seem as . . . far-fetched as being able to understand animals."

"Even if understanding animals is just another sense?"

He shrugged. "If it is, it's exceedingly rare."

I frowned at him. "Rare doesn't mean impossible, does it?"

"Well, no, but it's much more difficult to understand, let alone define," Dr. Robinson said. "Let alone believe."

And it was at that moment, in that hospital, that I realized maybe I had been too concerned with proof myself. That maybe evidence wasn't the only reason to believe that something might be true.

CHAPTER TWENTY-THREE

We collected my mother and James from the zoo before we went for Buster.

"You should have seen the elephants." James turned to look back over the seat at me. "They were like giant gray pigs with long noses and long legs and really big ears."

"So nothing at all like pigs," I said.

"And there was a tiger that was skinny all over except his huge head. Big as a bushel basket. But he wouldn't even get up and roar. Just lay there huffing. Lazy dumb cat."

"A zoo is not a circus," my father said. "The animals aren't meant to perform, James."

"Then next time let's go to the circus. Though I did like the zebras. And the hippos. Which really were a lot like pigs, Annabelle."

And he went on like that for quite some time, all the way to the animal hospital, where Buster waited for us to retrieve him.

When we got there, we all trooped inside to hear what the doctor had to say.

"Buster McBride, yes?" the woman at the desk asked.

"Yes," my father replied.

We waited while she went away and, after a bit, came back with a doctor whose badge said he was Dr. Bloom.

He didn't smell like a flower. He smelled far too clean to be anything wild.

And he didn't look like a flower, either. He had parched brown hair, eyebrows that looked so much like caterpillars that I expected them to crawl off his forehead, and a thick, shiny scar that ran down one side of his face.

But none of that mattered as much as his kind eyes and soft voice when he said, "Buster has a severely bruised spine."

After a moment, Henry asked, "Will it mend?"

The doctor sighed. "It already is mending, but I don't know if Buster will ever be able to walk again like he did, on all fours."

Henry stood there quietly, his chest rising and falling as he breathed in the news, his eyes busy as he thought it through. "What about the rest of it?"

"The rest of it?" The doctor focused on Henry so completely that I felt invisible, which was quite a change, and I tried not to mind.

And then I tried not to mind that I minded.

"Either way," Henry said, "whether he can walk or not, will he keep hurting the way he does now?"

The doctor sighed again. "That's hard to say. Probably not. If he heals enough to walk again, he may still have some pain for as long as he lives. The poor kid got hit hard." The doctor paused, his eyes on Henry. "If he stays paralyzed, he shouldn't feel anything past the bruise, but all kinds of other things can go wrong when a body loses so much function. And some of those things can cause pain. Even death."

Henry nodded. "Can he come home now?"

"Yes, he can. His back's not broken, so he doesn't need to be kept completely still, but he does need rest." The doctor hesitated. "Think of the worst bruise you've ever had, and then multiply that by ten. You can't see this one, but it's like a fist around his spinal cord, and it needs to relax before he'll be able to feel anything below it. So you'll have to work hard to keep him calm."

"And hope he'll walk again."

"Yes."

We listened for a while to other ways we would have to care for Buster.

"We can do those things," my mother said, though we knew it wouldn't be easy.

Dr. Bloom turned to me. "Dr. Peck said you were a special girl who could . . . communicate with animals."

I nodded. "Since I got struck by lightning."

Dr. Bloom smiled just a little. "If it sticks, you might want to think about becoming a doctor like me."

I wondered why he was so matter-of-fact about a lightning strike that had left me amazingly changed. "Have you known someone else who was struck by lightning?"

To which Dr. Bloom nodded. "Me. Though all I got from it was a scar and a decade in hospitals."

His scar, in the bright, interior light, looked like a glossy strap.

"Do you think you would have become a doctor otherwise?"

Dr. Bloom smiled. "I doubt it." He looked at my father. "You have interesting children, Mr. McBride."

My father nodded. "You have no idea."

Dr. Bloom turned to me. "Would you mind having a word with some of the other dogs in the hospital? It would help me to know more about what's wrong with them."

Which made me feel taller, and smarter, and eager to hear what the dogs had to say.

The others followed as I set out to make the rounds with Dr. Bloom.

If not for the fresh cedar shavings in every crate, the awful stench of urine would have been too much for me.

As it was, I struggled to put the smell aside. To focus on the dogs themselves as we walked from one cage to the next.

I told the doctor that the dachshund that wouldn't stop growling had a lump in his throat. "It feels like he swallowed something halfway." I tapped my throat.

The doctor looked at me, looked at the dog. "That's why he's growling?"

I nodded. "He's trying to clear it, but it won't clear."

The doctor raised his eyebrows. "All right. What about this poodle?"

We stepped along to the next big cage, my parents and Henry and James trailing along behind, all of them listening, watching.

I'd only ever seen little poodles, now and then, when town ladies came to market for peaches and lima beans. This one was a giant of a poodle the color of brown sugar, curly all over, of course, with a gleam of both intelligence and pain in her eyes. She lay in the crate and didn't even lift her head when I stopped before her, but after a moment, she whined.

Dr. Bloom waited. I peered more closely at the dog. "Her head hurts."

It was clear from the look on his face that Dr. Bloom had not really believed me before but that he believed me now.

"Right on both counts," he said softly. After a moment, he led us all past several more crates, to the back of the room, where another sat apart from the rest, in a dark corner. "I knew what was wrong with the others. And I apologize if that seemed like a trick. But this dog has me baffled. He won't eat. Won't drink. He's listless. Seems exhausted but doesn't sleep much, whether because he can't or won't, I don't know."

The dog in the cage was a young mutt, quite small and thin, with a dull coat, perhaps from what ailed him.

He lay on the floor of the crate, facing away from us, toward the wall.

"Is he a city dog?" Henry asked.

Dr. Bloom shrugged. "I would imagine so. He came to us from the pound, which is apt to put down a stray after two weeks if no one adopts him. And of course no one wanted a dog that lacked interest in anything at all, so this one was about at the end of things. But he's young and a nice enough lad. So they asked if I could sort him out."

"Hey, boy," Henry said softly, crouching low.

The dog didn't stir. Didn't make a sound.

I said, "Can I go in there with him?"

Dr. Bloom glanced at my father.

"If he's not dangerous," my father said.

"Annabelle," my mother said, "is that really necessary?"

"When I was a baby and I was sick, what did you do with me?"

My mother shrugged. "I held you."

I opened the door to the crate and crawled inside.

The dog paid some attention to that, shifting away, but I couldn't tell why. I felt very little from him.

But then I took him in my arms, there in that dark crate, and held him close against my chest.

He felt like silence. Like an absence. Nothing but emptiness. And a deep sorrow.

I wouldn't have *felt* such things without some help from the lightning, but I reckoned that I might have *known* them, regardless. Just as I knew something important as I looked at the others through the mesh of the crate.

The world looked very different from the inside than it had from the outside, and I could understand why the tiger had declined to roar.

"Well?" said Dr. Bloom.

"He's sad."

"Sad?"

"Sad." I thought about it. "Lonely."

My mother said, "Can sadness make a dog sick?"

Dr. Bloom waggled his head. "Sadness can be very hard on a body. In any kind of creature."

"Maybe he misses home," Henry said.

Which is when the dog turned toward me for the first time, the light from across the room touching his face.

"I know where home is," I said.

CHAPTER TWENTY-FOUR

"You're late," Aunt Lily groused when we pulled up in front of the museum. But she found something else to complain about as she climbed into the car. "*Two* dogs?!"

"We found Andy's at the hospital." I could hear, in my voice, the same joy I imagined on Andy's face when he saw his pup again. When his pup saw him.

"How do you know this is Andy's mutt?" Aunt Lily asked. "And why would you want to put an innocent creature back into the arms of that bully boy? And how is it any of our business in the first place?"

"He has one white eye, just like Andy's dog—"

"Well, surely there's more than one dog with a white eye," she said as my father pulled out into the traffic and headed for home.

But before I could respond, Aunt Lily began to argue with James about which was better, a hippo or a Van Gogh (and whether the mummy in the Egyptian exhibit would come to life when the sun went down)—and I turned my own attention to the dog in my lap.

He quivered with alarm as we made our way through the loud, chaotic city, but he grew eager and excited as we headed toward land he knew.

I felt much the same.

I'd been muddled about the confusions of my life and what I'd been born with and what the lightning had given me—whether I'd been changed or just woken up—and whether it mattered. Which was more important: what came from the inside or what came from the outside. And what to trust. More than anything, what to trust.

But as we rode along toward home, I decided once again not to worry so much about the things I couldn't understand or control or change or manage.

I decided to concentrate on what I *could*, instead.

And I would start with the dog in my lap.

I ran my hand over his ears, again and again, wondering what Andy called him.

If he'd been my dog, I'd have named him Eeyore for all that sorrow welling up inside him, though I hoped that would change when he saw Andy again.

How odd that he should be lonely for such a boy. But he knew things I didn't know. And he had his reasons for how he felt. Just as I had mine.

The dog tucked his face into the crook of my neck and sighed deeply.

My back ached a bit with the effort of holding him against me as the car rumbled along, but I was happy to be what he needed.

Regardless of what other tongues I understood, sadness was a language I knew.

"Will you let me off at the bridge again?" I asked my father. "So I can take this boy home to Andy?"

Aunt Lily turned to look over the seat at me. "And who will do the chores you've left undone?"

My mother started to say something, but I had my answer ready. "I will. Just as soon as I get home, which will be soon enough." I turned to my mother. "Is that okay?"

"Perfectly," she replied.

"I'd come with you," Henry said, "but I need to look after Buster."

I nodded. "It's all right. I'm fine on my own."

My father pulled over at the bridge over Wheeler's Run, and I climbed out, Andy's dog following me, and we started toward the Woodberry farm as the car dwindled away down the bottom road.

The nurse in Pittsburgh had given me a collar and an old leash to keep the dog close by, and I was glad of it now, for he pulled toward home the way an ox will pull a wagon, leaning into it, his head down, flexing his shoulders and pawing the dust.

"Easy, boy!" I yelped, tugging him back gently . . . but then giving in and loping along behind him as he hurried toward what he knew and what he'd missed and what was nearly his again.

And I thought about how a desire became stronger the closer it got to its reward.

When we reached the farm, Andy was nowhere to be seen.

"Andy!" I called, the dog whining and yipping as he paced to the end of the leash and back again.

"ANDY!" I called again, louder, one hand cupped to steer my voice, the other clinging to the leash.

After a long moment, Andy stepped out of a barn on the far side of the pasture, wiping his hands on a rag.

He peered into the distance toward us, and even from so far away I could see him go still. Drop the rag. Stand straight for a moment, leaning toward us. And then begin to run.

I knelt quickly, untied the leash, and let the dog go.

He sailed over the gully, bounded through the tall grass on the far side, scooted under the wire fence, and then took off in a blur, his paws barely touching the ground, flying over rocks and tree stumps like a stone skipped across a pond.

While Andy (who seemed a sloth at school, draping himself over his desk, snoozing, disdainful of us all) likewise ran, calling a name I would never have imagined as he thundered across the pasture. "Spud!" he cried, again and again.

I waited by the road as they tumbled together onto the ground, rolling happily in the grass while the cows nearby paused in their grazing to watch.

"So," I said quietly to myself. "So."

I waited, my eyes on them, until Andy stood up, Spud making figure eights around his legs.

Andy looked across the pasture at me for a long, long moment.

I looked steadily back.

And then, to my surprise, Andy turned and walked again toward the barn, the dog leaping and twisting at his side.

He must have had questions.

Why hadn't he come to ask them? Why hadn't he come to thank me?

But there was time for that. And I hadn't cared about thanks until it wasn't given.

I left it behind as they disappeared into the barn and I turned toward home.

Watching their reunion would be the thing I took away with me that day. And kept.

CHAPTER TWENTY-FIVE

I couldn't pass by the Edelman place without letting Nora
know what we'd learned in Pittsburgh, and why we weren't
taking Buster back to her.

This time, Mr. Edelman's truck was in the lane.

As I crossed the gulley onto his land, the dogs set up
a ruckus that brought him out of the house and onto the
front porch, a napkin tucked into his collar.

He glared at me as I walked closer, my heart thumping
even though I knew his bark was worse than his bite.

"What do you want?" he said without a trace of welcome.

"Hello, Mr. Edelman." I realized that I was still in my
church dress from the trip into the city, and that I must
have looked odd standing there.

He frowned suspiciously. "How do you know my name?
And what's yours?"

"I'm Annabelle McBride. And if Miss . . . if Nora is at home, I would like to speak with her for a moment." I sounded like a schoolmarm.

His eyebrows went up. "Nora?"

And I realized that she hadn't told him about me. "Your daughter. Nora."

"I know who my daughter is," he growled, glaring at me, though with the napkin hanging from his collar he looked like a big, grizzled baby. "How is it that *you* know her?"

At which Nora came out through the door behind him. "Hello, Annabelle." To her father, she said, "She and her brother Henry came looking for his dog. That mutt you hit in the storm."

The news stood him up straight. He looked at me with a little less glare in his eye. "Which I did not mean to do. The little fool ran right out in front of me."

I didn't appreciate the *fool*, but I could imagine that hitting Buster must have been an awful thing for them both. And I knew that even the best people sometimes looked for someone to blame when things went wrong.

"So what did the veterinarian in Pittsburgh say?" Nora asked.

"You took him to a vet?" Mr. Edelman said. "In Pittsburgh? And spent good money to find out that the dog either will heal or won't?" He turned to his daughter. "You let them do that?"

"I did. It makes a difference, knowing how to treat him. I would have told you, but I knew you'd act just like you're acting."

"And we spent nothing but a little time," I said. "I made a deal with the doctors: They could examine me if they also examined my brother's dog."

More befuddlement. "You don't look sick."

"Not sick. But I got struck by lightning in that same storm, and now I can understand dogs."

Mr. Edelman stood up a bit straighter. "Anyone who's paying attention can understand dogs."

And I knew he wasn't wrong. But Nora shook her head. "Not like Annabelle can."

"Well," said Mr. Edelman, "then why go all the way to Pittsburgh to find out what's wrong with him?"

Which sounded like he believed me . . . evidence or not.

"I'm not a doctor. I knew his back hurt, but I didn't know why."

Nora sighed impatiently. "So what did the doctor say?"

I told them about the bruise on Buster's spine.

"But he wasn't sure if Buster will recover?" Nora asked.

I shook my head. "At least his spine isn't *broken*. We would have brought him back so you could look after him properly, but we couldn't think of a way to explain why we would come back here instead of taking Buster home again. We didn't want to make trouble for you."

Mr. Edelman looked thoughtfully at his daughter, but he didn't say anything.

After a bit, Nora sighed again. "If you need to bring him back, you should do that, Annabelle. Perhaps without a whole passel of people, but whatever's best for Buster. That would be all right."

I nodded. "I'll let you know."

Mr. Edelman leaned again the porch rail. "That must have been quite an adventure, meeting those doctors."

"It was. But the best part was when we found the lost dog from the farm next door."

They both stared at me. "With one white eye?" Nora said. "The one that's been missing for weeks?"

"The same."

"Where was he?"

"At the animal hospital." Then I told them about how I had translated for the dogs so the doctor would know what ailed them.

While I talked, Nora settled herself in one of the rocking chairs, Mr. Edelman in the other, and I sat sideways on one of the porch steps.

When I got to the part about the brown-sugar poodle, a house finch swooped in and hovered just above us, her chicks craning their necks from the nest wedged in an elbow of porch trim, their yellow beaks gaping open like blossoms.

"It's nice of you to let them nest here," I said.

"Not a matter of *let*." Mr. Edelman made a go-on motion with his hand. "So, the poodle?"

And I went on, telling them about that and then about finding Spud.

"Fascinating," Mr. Edelman said. "And a little hard to believe."

I didn't blame him for having doubts.

And then I told them the last bit, about how I had taken Spud home to Andy. How they had met again in the pasture.

"A dog will get in a truck, from time to time," Mr. Edelman said. "Like the big Dodge that comes to the Woodberrys' to pick up milk. And find himself far from home. Have to start again." He looked sad—even stricken—at the thought.

I remembered what I'd first thought about Mr. Edelman. That he was mean, or worse.

I frowned at him. "I need to apologize," I said slowly.

He raised his eyebrows. "What for?"

"When I saw you drive by in your truck the other day, I thought you were mean."

Nora huffed at that. "And who could blame you? That's how he acts."

"I do indeed."

"But acting like something and being something

aren't always the same thing." And I felt the echo between what I'd said and what Nora had said when we'd first met her. About the difference between *seems to be* and *is*. "Though sometimes they are."

Mr. Edelman chuckled. "You're very decisive."

I dipped my head. "I keep trying to see past what I can see, but it's hard."

"And some of us need to put on a better face," Nora said.

"What's wrong with my face?" he said.

She laughed. "You're terrifying. I'm surprised Annabelle had the grit to come knocking, with you here."

I liked the idea that I had grit. That I was tough.

But then I thought again about my father's soft heart. And wondered whether mine was too hard sometimes.

"I'm sorry about my face," Mr. Edelman said to me.

"And I'm sorry I thought you were mean," I replied.

He held out his hand. "So we're even?"

I reached out and took his hand.

It was as hard and bony and rough as a bundle of sticks. As rough as the hand I'd felt on my face after I'd been knocked down in the storm. But I couldn't be sure they were the same, though it was easy to imagine Mr. Edelman roaming around the hills, looking for animals to save. Finding me, instead.

I wanted to ask him, and Nora as well, but if either of them had saved me, surely they would have said as much.

Which led me back to the question: Why would someone do such a good thing and not say so?

"I know you don't want to be bothered, but helping those dogs is a kindness," I said. "There are lots of people who would thank you for doing that."

"Don't need any thanks." Mr. Edelman frowned. "And we get plenty from the dogs."

"Besides," Nora said sternly, "don't forget what I told you, Annabelle. The people who hurt those dogs ought not to know where they are. Especially that Mr. Graf."

Her father squinted at her. "Who's that?"

"Mr. Graf," I said, surprised that Nora hadn't already told him the story. "He's looking for that bull terrier you have. Zeus."

"Mercy," Mr. Edelman said, but he didn't seem overly concerned. "A girl struck by lightning and a dog named for a thunder god. Maybe Thor can come by next and hammer the crooked out of this porch."

Which made me laugh.

Which pleased Mr. Edelman.

Which made me think there wasn't much laughter in his house.

We talked about the dogs for a while longer.

And then I asked the Edelmans why they'd come to live way out in the hills.

Nora hesitated for a moment. "We were sick of the

city. Too much noise. Air all fogged up with smoke and soot and gas and who knows what. Everything getting ground up and spit out. Like living in a pepper mill."

I had thought the same thing myself, just that morning, though the city was exciting, too.

I waited for Mr. Edelman to speak his piece, but he just rocked quietly, gazing at his daughter, a mighty tenderness in his eyes.

And I knew that Nora had told the truth: He had come here not for the dogs, not for the countryside, but for her.

To help her get over something. That part seemed clear. And to help her toward something better.

"We were just having a late lunch, and there's plenty if you want some, Annabelle." Mr. Edelman climbed to his feet. "Small payment for such good stories."

Nora held the screen door open.

I hesitated for a moment—remembering my chores, my promise to be home soon—but then decided to stay.

They were an odd pair, the Edelmans. And I still wasn't sure what to make of them. But I wanted to know them better.

So in I went.

CHAPTER TWENTY-SIX

The Edelman house was a surprise. Full of books, a phonograph even finer than Aunt Lily's, cut flowers, and pictures of a woman so beautiful that I didn't know where else to look but at her.

"My mother," Nora said quietly. They looked alike.

"Where is she?" I asked without thinking.

Nora turned away. "She died just a year ago."

Mr. Edelman pulled out a chair at the table and waved me toward it. "Don't be shy. Come join us. You must be hungry after the day you've had."

I sat down. They sat. We looked at each other in silence.

Nora offered me a basket of rolls and a bowl of egg salad with chopped pickles.

Somewhere, a clock marched through its seconds in sharp little heels.

One of the dogs barked in the distance.

I thought about the animal hospital in the city. All its caged dogs.

This place felt much as it had. Not just the barn but the house, too.

"How did she die?" I asked before I had a chance to stop myself.

Mr. Edelman put down his iced tea.

Nora cleared her throat.

Neither of them looked at me.

"She died in a train wreck," Nora said.

Mr. Edelman sat stiff in his chair, every muscle tense, as if he were locked up tight with no key at all.

"We were on our way to visit my grandmother, in Ohio." Nora folded her napkin in half. In quarters. "I had the window seat so I could watch the world go by. If I'd been in the aisle seat, I would have been the one to die."

As it was, Nora had watched her mother fade away while the people around them screamed and scrabbled to get free.

Not a single one had stopped to help.

Nora talked about that. The way the other passengers had shoved and jostled their way past, climbing over fallen luggage, fallen people, desperate to get out, while Nora had knelt alongside her mother, trying to help her, trying to hear what she was whispering, failing at both.

"I'm so sorry," I said, the tears coming, mostly for Nora and her father but then for Toby, too, and for me. I knew how it felt to be helpless, though I hadn't lost my mother. "I know what it's like to try."

Nora frowned at me, wiping her eyes. "But you're so young."

As if that had anything to do with anything. "So are you."

She flapped a hand tiredly. "I don't feel young."

I didn't either as I imagined what Nora carried with her, day after day.

And I decided they would both understand about Toby, so I told them. About what he'd been like, both before I'd known him and after I'd come to be his friend. About how Betty had set out to ruin him. "I tried to help him, but I think I made things worse along the way."

"Makes no sense to think like that," Nora said, her voice trembling a little. "Though I do know why . . ."

And then she suddenly drifted off, the words trailing away, her eyes staring at nothing, her face pale, her hands beginning to twitch.

"Is she all right?" I said, drying my cheeks with my hands.

Mr. Edelman nodded. "She will be. But it's best you go now, Annabelle, so she can get some rest." He stood up and went around the table to wrap an arm around his daughter and pull her snug against him. "She just needs some rest."

Something was wrong, but I didn't know what, or whether it had something to do with Nora's memories, though I supposed it did.

"Good-bye," I said quietly, tucking in my chair.

He walked me to the door.

"She's not as prickly as she seems," he said softly, glancing back over his shoulder.

I found that surprising, coming from a man like him.

"It's been hard for her since her mother died, and much more you don't know about. Life so far has not always been kind to Nora." He sighed. "My wife used to say that we can't go wrong if we figure everyone we meet is carrying a bushel of rocks. Whether we can see it or not."

I stared at him. "A bushel of rocks?"

"Something too heavy for one person to manage."

I pondered that. "Nora told me you're a scientist."

"A geneticist. What of it?" He seemed a bit put out, that I would bring it up.

"I'm sorry," I said. "I was just—"

"No need to be sorry, Annabelle." He bowed his head in apology. "I just . . . well, I've given that up for a little while, and I'm trying hard not to miss it."

"But why give it up? You have a whole farm here."

"No laboratory. No way to keep the wind and the bugs from pollinating things however they like. So I've taken a sabbatical." At the look on my face, he said, "Some time off. To do other things."

He glanced toward Nora and back.

And I saw again an extraordinary tenderness in his eyes.

CHAPTER TWENTY-SEVEN

I thought about the Edelmans as I headed for home, eager to change out of my church dress and do my chores.

Nothing like good, simple work to lift a darkness. Like feeding the chickens or hanging wash, my hands doing what they knew how to do while my head figured itself out and my heart found its way.

But as I walked along the road, I heard my name and stopped, looking around until I heard it again.

"Annabelle!"

I glanced back and saw, in the near distance, a boy coming toward me, a dog alongside him.

I waited, watching the small things that set the boy apart from everyone else: the way he walked, how he held his head tipped just slightly to one side. The angle of his hat. His habit of plucking a leaf from a bush as he passed.

Andy.

I waited where I was.

Even from a distance I could feel Spud's joy.

And from the way Andy was walking, I could tell that he was happy, too, though it didn't show on his face.

When he got close enough, he said, "What's with the dress?" Which made me feel ridiculous. "And where did you find my dog?" It was like he was made out of sandpaper.

I decided to make him wait.

"What's his name?" I asked, though I'd already heard him calling to Spud from across the cow pasture.

Andy scowled at me. "Spud. His name's Spud. What about it?"

"Like a potato?"

"Of course like a potato. I asked where you found him."

After a moment, I said, "We went to Pittsburgh this morning. To an animal hospital. And Spud was there."

The surprise on his face was almost comical. "That's twenty-five miles from here!"

I nodded. "He was a long way from home. Mr. Edelman said maybe he got into a milk truck and ended up in the city by mistake."

Andy raised his eyebrows. "One minute you don't know who Edelman is, and the next minute you're talking to him about my dog?"

I nearly said, *Because of Nora*, but I caught myself. "Henry and I went to ask him if he'd seen Buster."

"And why were you at an animal hospital in Pittsburgh in the first place?"

So I told him some of the story. Not all of it. Just the parts about Mr. Edelman hitting Buster with his truck.

"And you went all the way to the city? For a mutt like that?"

I stood up straighter. "We did. And I'm surprised at you, Andy. The way you act about Spud, I'd expect you to understand such a thing."

He stared at me for a long moment. "Who said I don't?"

And I was more confused than ever.

I stared back at him, trying to see past all the things I'd already seen. "Why did you come looking for me?"

"Looking for *you*?" He huffed at that. "Don't flatter yourself."

At which I felt terribly stupid. But there were worse things than stupid.

"I don't know why I bother talking to you at all," I said.

The disappointment I felt, after watching him in that cow pasture with Spud, was a fresh, unwelcome hurt.

For a long moment, he just looked at me. Then he sighed and stared off across the field of corn that stretched between the road and Wheeler's Run.

"We're missing a cow. My pa thinks I left the gate open, but I didn't." He touched his swollen nose. "And even if I did, which I didn't, cows don't stray much, and if they do, they're easy to spot. Or people bring them back. But she's gone."

So he hadn't been out looking for me, and I wasn't sure whether to feel glad or not. "You're out looking for a *cow*?"

He nodded. "An old-timer. Nearly dry, so I know my pa planned to butcher her. Not much meat around here these days." He gave a rough bark of laughter. "Maybe she knew what was coming and hit the road, but it wasn't me left the gate open. Though someone did. Must have, for Honk to get loose like that."

I frowned at him. "Honk?"

He looked at me expectantly, though I had no idea why. "You know, *Honk*," he finally said, a bit pink in the cheeks. "Like the moose."

Honk the Moose had been one of my favorite books when I was smaller. My mother sometimes still read it to James, especially when he was sick.

But no matter how hard I tried, I couldn't imagine who might have read it to Andy.

As if he could hear my thoughts, he said, "My grandma used to read it to me." He looked at his boots.

I remembered her funeral. Andy must have been about nine at the time. Maybe ten.

"I was looking for Honk," he suddenly said. "Not you." And his voice was as cold as ever.

I recalled the lowing of a cow from somewhere in Wolf

Hollow—how lonely she had sounded—and I wanted to tell Andy that maybe I could help him find his lost Honk, but I didn't.

Instead, I turned without another word and walked away.

When I looked back after a while, Andy was gone.

I'd intended to cut through the corn and into the woods, along one of the many paths that led from the bottomland up the long hill to home, but the potato house was just a bit farther along, so I kept going that way instead.

It was as we'd left it, my father and I, except that this time, when I looked for it, there was no rubber ball tucked under the edge of the burlap pallet.

Andy had come back since we'd been here.

I pictured him bringing Spud to the potato house sometime soon, the two of them watching the flight of the moon through the open window.

For a few long moments, I stood in the hot little house and thought about what it would look like if I fixed it up.

I imagined sweeping it clean, the broom damp to keep the dust down. Washing the windows inside and out. Bringing in a proper bed. A small table to put alongside it. A lantern on the table. A bit of rug on the floor.

My musings took me as far as a Mason jar full of wildflowers before I stopped myself.

Andy had been a bully for a long time. Showed signs that he still was. Promised to be one again, straight through his life.

The love of a dog didn't change that. Nor did a cow named Honk.

I'd have to be careful to remember what I knew about Andy. All of it. Even as I looked for what I'd forgotten. Or could not so easily see.

CHAPTER TWENTY-EIGHT

I woke the next morning to rain, the wind lugging heavy sacks of cloud across the sky, the trees dressed in clothes too drab for June.

I was grateful, really. We needed frequent rain. For the crops. To top up the well. To keep the dust down.

But indoor chores would keep me housebound, and I had things I wanted to do, further afield.

So I jumped into my work as soon as I saw the colors of the day, helping with breakfast, the ironing, the endless battle against dust and pollen and mud, while Henry tended to Buster, and James and my father and my grandpap went out to the barn to finish grinding the corn.

"That's enough," my mother finally said after we'd put away all the clean wash. "You go on and see how Henry's doing with that dog of his."

So I tried to help my brother change Buster's soiled bandages without hurting him—though we made a mess of things despite our best efforts—and then settled him in an old blanket gathered nest-like in our Radio Flyer on the porch. It was a good little wagon, if a bit beat up from all the times we'd tried to ride it down the lane only to skid and tumble in the gravel. But it still had four good tires and more red than rust.

"You can pull him around in that if you watch for bumps," I said.

Henry sighed. "He looks foolish."

"Oh, fiddle. He's a dog. He doesn't care how he looks."

And it was true. He didn't care. All he really wanted was Henry. And to feel better.

"He looks like the world's ugliest baby," Henry said. "All swaddled up. Hunter will laugh at him."

I turned to Hunter, who was lying in a corner of the porch, out of the rain. "You wouldn't laugh at Buster, would you?"

He replied with a sloppy grin and a slow blink before settling into his nap, and I felt warm and safe and whole.

"Look, Henry, I know you want Buster here with you, but I think we should take him back to Nora. Unless you plan to spend every waking moment by his side, cleaning up after him, fretting about whether he's getting better or worse." They both looked worn out already, and there was a long way to go. "Nora knows what she's doing. And you can visit him every day."

Henry sighed. "I know. And not because I don't want to take care of him. Because I do."

"I know you do. But she's best for him while he's still healing. I'm just not sure how to explain things to Daddy and Mother and keep our promise to Nora, all at the same time."

"I don't see how she can hide forever," Henry said. "Not in a township as small as this one."

He was right, but I reckoned it was up to Nora. Maybe her father. Not us.

"I'll go on down there first," I said, "and see what she wants us to do."

When I told my mother I was going out, she looked at me like I'd taken leave of my senses. "A walk? On a day like this?"

"I won't melt. And it's not thundering. I wouldn't go out if it were."

She'd been slicing carrots for stew, but now she pointed the knife at me. "Any hint of storm, and you get yourself home. Or stay where you are, if it's under a good roof. Do you understand?"

"I promise." But I hadn't taken two steps before she called me back.

"And what's so important that it can't wait for the rain to stop?"

She looked suspicious, and I really couldn't blame her, so I told her part of the truth, even though it was as prickly as anything else I might have said, maybe more.

"Andy's lost a cow and I thought she might have wandered our way."

That surprised her. "First your father lets him sleep in the potato house, then you hand-deliver his missing dog, and now you're headed out into the slop to look for his cow?"

I shrugged. "I like the idea of finding a lost cow. Doesn't matter whose it is. And her name is Honk. Like *Honk the Moose*."

She stared at me as if I'd grown horns. "Do you speak cow, too?"

"Maybe a little."

As she turned back to her work, she muttered something that sounded like *circus*. But I couldn't be sure.

I put on my rain boots and an old poncho that made me feel like a bell and headed out into the wet, enjoying the brown batter of mud under my feet and the rain popping on my hood.

As I walked, I spent some time on Andy's story. About how his cow had gone missing.

Cows couldn't climb fences or fly away.

If Andy hadn't left the gate open, someone else had.

And if one cow had gone astray, why not others?

But I set that puzzle aside as I reached the top of the lane and, instead of going over the crest of the hill and down the path toward the schoolhouse, headed for an old red pine forest my great-grandparents had planted long before I was born.

It was a strange bit of woods, all in rows, with nothing much growing in its shadows. But I loved how quiet it was there as I slipped along on the wet pine needles, easing downhill from the regiment of orderly pines into an old and twisted apple orchard lost to the wilderness, no more fruit here except the occasional dimpled stray that didn't even tempt the birds.

I loved the spongy dampness of the abandoned apple trees, the white-green-black scabs of lichen on their knobby trunks, the wonderful, refreshing rot of their mushy branches and freckled leaves.

And I felt quite happy as I walked along in the misty rain, alone on land I knew almost to the inch.

"Honk!" I called now and then as I walked, mostly for the fun of it, feeling like a goose.

But as I cut down along a deer path toward the bottomland, I heard what was unmistakably a moo.

I stopped and held still, pulled off my hood, and let the rain have its way.

There. Once again.

A moo.

Just an ordinary moo. No panic in it, though I gathered that the cow was . . . confused.

Lost, I thought. That would explain it.

But if she were Andy's cow, why was she still lost, especially so close to home? Not more than half a mile or so, though to get where she was, she would have had to cross Wheeler's Run. Not an easy thing for a cow, the rocks slippery, dangerous for a creature with hooves.

Either that or she'd come the long way, by the road, but in that case someone would have seen her and taken her in.

Another moo.

It seemed to be coming from the Turtle Stone, a huge boulder that sat in the middle of a clearing in the woods, huge and smooth and reliable. As permanent as a small planet. The leaves of the surrounding sugar maples like stars in its galaxy.

It was a place where I had often gone to sort out what puzzled me, though not since Betty and Andy had spent time there, plotting their mischief.

I'd been afraid to find that it had changed. That they had changed it.

But then I heard another moo, and I set out toward the clearing to see what I could see.

CHAPTER TWENTY-NINE

The Turtle Stone was right where it was supposed to be, the clearing spread all over with white and purple violets, as if the woods had chosen to plant no saplings here, the stone and the flowers worth their bit of land, too.

I had stayed away long enough. Whatever Betty and Andy had done here had been cast away by the violets and the silence.

And by the cow I found standing alongside the Turtle Stone.

I edged closer, speaking to her softly. "Easy, girl. You're all right now."

And she *was* all right.

Someone had tied her to a sturdy tree at the edge of the clearing, but with enough rope so she could wander a bit and graze on violets and grasses. And there was a clump of hay, too, and a bucket of water, which was overflowing from the rain.

"Good girl," I crooned, easing closer, my hand out until I was close enough for her to plant her big, square nose in it.

"That tickles," I said at the touch of her whiskers, smiling at her lovely eyes.

She bowed her head a little so I could scratch between her ears.

Andy had said she was an old cow, nearly dry, and he'd been right. But she still needed a bit of milking, so I knelt alongside her and gave her some ease, the milk disappearing into the soggy ground, nothing but white bubbles left behind.

I stood up, brushed myself off, and assessed the situation.

Someone had led an old cow away from home, through the woods, and tied her up in a place where she was likely to escape notice for quite some time.

Even her mooing wouldn't seem terribly odd.

Our own cows were confined to a few acres around our barn, but their mooing didn't obey the fences we'd put up, and the sound of them and others nearby was common in these hills. The same was true of other cows, in other glens.

So people were a bit immune to the background music of our days: cows mooing, crows bickering, and the endless bugs, tuning their instruments, fiddling for mates.

But I had been looking for a missing cow, so I had paid a different kind of attention.

I considered what I knew and what I didn't know, including who might have brought her here.

I imagined what Nora might do at the idea that an old cow would be slaughtered after a lifetime of service.

She'd save such a cow. I knew she would. Same as I would. Same as anyone would, who'd tried and failed before to save something or someone worth saving.

I reckoned that Nora might have stumbled across the Turtle Stone while exploring the countryside, getting her bearings and looking for strays. But I couldn't imagine her leaving a cow tied up alone in the woods, even during the warm days of June. And Nora had to know that she couldn't possibly rescue every farm animal that faced its turn with the butcher.

I could think of only one other person who might have saved this old cow.

Just a few days earlier, I might have tried harder to find another answer. One that made more sense.

But I knew more now than I'd known then.

The old cow gazed at me, her coat dark with rain, drops gathering along her ears, her long eyelashes. She shook her head a bit, and the water from her coat flicked against my face.

"Let's get you somewhere warm and dry," I said,

struggling to untie the wet rope from the tree.

I left the hay and the bucket for whatever deer might come through after we'd left.

And I led the old cow along the path from the Turtle Stone, up the hill toward home, and then along a tractor lane at the crest, around toward the far end of our glen. I aimed to come up on the barn from the back, away from the house, where no one would see me.

I could hear my father and grandpap and James on the threshing floor above as I led Honk into the lower, down-hill part of the barn, where there were stalls for the two horses and our own three cows, all of which were inside, sheltering from the rain.

"I've brought you some company," I told Daisy, the youngest of the Guernseys, as I opened the gate to her stall and led Honk in, roughing up her drenched coat with a handful of straw.

The stalls were roomy enough, and I knew cows were patient and amiable animals, so I was sure Daisy would share her feed and that the two would be fine together until I sorted out what came next.

Someone would find Honk soon enough, but for now she was safe and warm, with enough to eat and no reason to be scared or lonely anymore.

All of which added up to a lot, for a cow. For anyone.

CHAPTER THIRTY

I'd spent too much time on Honk to go to Nora's before my mother would need me for lunch, so I headed for the house, washing my boots in the long, wet grass as I went, hoping I wouldn't smell too much like cow by the time I reached the kitchen.

"You smell like a cow," my mother said when I joined her at the sink.

"I was in the barn, visiting with Daisy." Which was true.

She gestured with her chin. "After you wash up, get the table set and then go ring the bell."

My grandma came slowly through from the sitting room. "There's my girl." She held out her arms, and I stepped into them, tucking my head against her neck.

"I'm sorry if I smell like cow," I said, stepping away.

"Nothing wrong with that." She smiled tiredly. "Work always smells just fine to me."

And I knew she was wistful about how much she'd once done and how little she could do now.

I pulled out her chair and helped her into it, then I washed up and set the table before I went out to ring the bell.

I found Henry huddled on the porch swing next to Buster lying in his wagon bed, the two of them looking damp and forlorn.

"You're still out here?"

Hunter climbed to his feet and yawned at the sound of my voice.

"I don't want to leave Buster alone," Henry said, "but I don't want to jostle him too much, either."

"I haven't been down to Nora's yet, but I'll go after lunch. And we'll get Buster back to her soon as we can."

Hunter padded over and pushed his head against my knee, snorting a little. "Are you a goat or a pig?" I asked him.

But he didn't answer except to yawn again and wag his tail.

And then he wandered off the porch, out into the rain, and away.

I stood, watching him, cold, suddenly, from head to toe.

"Annabelle?" I turned to find Henry staring at me. "Are you all right?"

I watched Hunter as he made his way into the trees along the lane. "I'm fine."

But I wasn't fine.

Suddenly, inexplicably, Hunter was as he'd been before. A nice enough dog whose path I crossed from time to time. Nothing more.

And I, suddenly, inexplicably, was as I'd been before. A girl who loved dogs but had no idea what they were feeling. Not really. Not more than anyone else did.

It was gone, the new sense I'd had for a little while.

I gazed at Henry, this boy who'd always understood dogs far better than I. "Do you wish you had what the lightning gave me?"

I'd surprised him.

He mulled it over for a moment. "I suppose I do, though it's hard to say, since I can't feel what you feel, so I don't know how different we are, you and I. Or what I'm missing. Or what I'm not."

"You mean you already know dogs pretty well."

He nodded. "I reckon I do. From the look in their eyes. The way they are. From paying attention to them."

The way I had known Toby, though he'd said very little. Though other people had thought him frightening. Even dangerous. While I had not.

"But you would be sad if you'd had what I had and then lost it?" I could hear the regret in my voice.

Henry's face fell. "Have you lost it, Annabelle?"

When I didn't answer right away, he said in a quiet

voice, "I think I'd feel quite mournful if I had something like that and lost it. But I wouldn't be sorry that I'd had it in the first place."

I nodded. "I've lost it. The part with Hunter. That part of it, anyway." But then I looked back across the day. "And the rest, too, I think."

I thought my way through the chores with my mother, the moment on the porch with Hunter when I'd felt such comfort . . . hadn't that been him? I'd thought so. And then going out into the rain. The tang of the pines. The wonderful decay of those apple trees. What I'd decided about Honk, about who had left her at the Turtle Stone.

And I realized that every bit of it might well have come from me instead of the lightning. Even the smell of the woods, which depended on me being there. Which would have smelled different to a fox, or a deer, or a dog.

And more, besides. How Andy had longed for Spud, though he had worked so hard to seem indifferent. The agony of Nora's memories. What she'd felt as her mother slipped away. And Henry himself. This small, brave brother of mine, who now stared at me, his face as serious as I'd ever seen it.

"Maybe it will come back," he said.

"I doubt it. Dr. Peck said it could go away as quickly as it came. But it's all right, Henry." And I realized that it *was* all right. Better than all right. "It really is. I think what you said about those pigs was true. I think the lightning was just a reminder."

"Of what?"

"Of a lot of things I already knew but maybe didn't know I knew. Or forgot I knew. Or didn't think I could trust anymore. Which sounds confusing," I said at the look on his face. "I'm confused myself. But I think maybe it's better this way. To have it gone. To have what's left."

I leaned close to Buster. "How do you feel, boy?"

His answer was to reach out with his tongue, to kiss my hand.

I straightened up and gave myself a little shake. "Why don't you take Buster inside, Henry. But don't tell anyone about this."

"Why not?"

"Because I want to think about it."

And then I tugged on the bell rope two, three times, the sound shivering out across the distance to call the others in.

After they'd washed up, everyone sat down while my mother and I dished out the stew we'd made that morning, each bowl topped with a dumpling or two.

When I put my father's bowl in front of him, he looked up. "I don't suppose you'd know anything about a strange cow that managed to find its way into the barn?"

"Honk," I said, distracted.

Everyone stared at me.

"Honk?" my father said.

"You sound like a goose," James said. "Can you speak goose now?"

I fetched another bowl of stew. "Honk is the name of the cow."

"Like Honk the moose!" James crowed. "He snuck into a barn, too."

I nodded. "She's Andy's cow. She was lost, but I found her in Wolf Hollow."

I didn't say anything about the Turtle Stone, or that she'd been tied up there.

I didn't want to talk about it. Or about who had left her there. Or why. I wanted to think about it.

So I ate my stew and listened with half an ear to the others, lost in my thoughts, and tried to figure out what to do next.

CHAPTER THIRTY-ONE

By the time my mother and I had washed and dried and put away the lunch dishes, I'd made up my mind.

First, I would go to see Nora about taking Buster back. Then I would go to see Andy, to tell him I had Honk.

"I'll be home soon," I told my mother as I put on my rain gear again.

"Off to look for more stray cows?" she said, smiling.

When I didn't answer, she tipped my chin up and looked into my eyes. "Are you all right, Annabelle?"

"I am. Just a bit out of sorts. But I'll get myself back in sorts. I promise."

She tucked my hair under my hood. "I'm sure you will. And make sure you're home in time to finish your chores."

That much had not changed. Work was work. And there was more than enough to go around.

All the way to the Edelmans', I breathed in as deeply as I could, listened with all my might, kept my eyes wide open, and watched for whatever ought not to be missed.

I was happy when the rain smelled much as it always had before. When the touch of a sapling along the edge of the path felt as it had always felt. And when the Juneberries I plucked from a branch along Wheeler's Run were as sweet as they'd ever been. No more, but no less, either. Just right.

Mr. Edelman's truck was not in the lane.

"Nora!" I called from time to time as I headed down the Edelmans' lane, but she didn't answer, didn't come to the door when I knocked or appear at the big open mouth of the barn as I went on, calling her name.

The dogs were barking quite a lot. More than the last time I'd been there. Louder. And I could tell that they had something important to say.

I picked up my pace as I neared the barn, their voices weaving a thread of worry, twisting it around my throat and tugging harder and harder the closer I got.

And then there she was, lying on the threshing floor, her arms and legs jerking and twitching, her white skin whiter than ever.

I dropped to my knees beside her.

"Nora!" I cried, shaking her shoulder, but she was firmly in the grip of something awful.

I remembered how she had stared and twitched the day before, and I knew she was sick.

The dogs knew it, too. They all stood barking in their pens, staring at us, obviously worried. But they couldn't help her any more than I could.

"I'll be right back!" I promised, climbing to my feet and racing out of the barn, down the lane and into the house, straight to the telephone, which I grabbed off the wall, flicking the hook to alert Mrs. Gribble, but the line was dead.

I dropped the receiver and ran out into the yard.

Home was too far.

So I took off again, straight for the nearest help to be had.

When I reached the lane to Andy's house, I yelled his name as loud as I could, worried about going any closer to a place where I'd never been welcome, but then I sprinted down along the edge of the cow pasture, through the gate in the yard fence, and straight up to his house.

No geraniums here. No rocking chairs. No birds nesting. Just peeling paint, cracked windowpanes, dirt, and the stink of the cow barn. The gamey funk of the cheeseworks.

Spud appeared from a corner of the porch and came to stand with me, quaking a bit though he was dry and home, and I wondered if I reminded him of where he'd been for those long weeks without his boy.

"Andy!" I called, slapping the frame of the screen door with the flat of my hand.

After a moment, he appeared all at once.

Through the screen, he looked gray.

"*What?*" he hissed, glancing over his shoulder. "*What are you doing here?*"

I bent over, winded, my hands on my knees. "I need help. Something's wrong with Nora."

He leaned a little closer but didn't open the door. "Who's Nora?"

And I remembered that he didn't know. "She's Mr. Edelman's daughter." I straightened up. "There's something wrong with her."

"He has a daughter?"

"I tried to call Dr. Peck, but their line is dead!"

He shook his head. "Ours is, too. Pulled down in the storm, and it's not fixed yet."

"Then come with me. Please! I think she might be dying."

"Annabelle, I can't. I'm—"

"Andy, she's in trouble!" I pulled on the screen door, but he pulled back, jumping when it slammed shut again.

"Annabelle, *hush*! My mother's sleeping, and—"

From somewhere close by I heard Andy's mother call

his name. She sounded angry in a way I'd never heard before. Not from a mother.

Even through the screen, I could see his eyes widen, his face fall.

"ANDY!" she yelled, louder this time.

And he was gone, as if he'd never been there in the first place.

I was glad I couldn't see what happened next. Hearing it was bad enough.

The fury in his mother's voice. Andy's own voice, so meek it didn't sound like his. Then the sound of her slap, which made me jump while Spud cringed behind my legs, and I wondered how often he might have felt her boot.

Andy reappeared at the door. Through the screen, his eyes were like holes.

"You'd better get on back to her yourself," he said in a flat voice. "Find someone else to help you."

"But won't you come with me?"

He gave me a long look, and I was reminded of the one he'd given me across the pasture when I'd brought Spud home. This one, too, was full of questions. But these were of a darker sort.

"I can't." He glanced over his shoulder. Turned back toward me.

I stayed where I was.

"Annabelle, I can't."

I waited.

And then I saw the beginning of something different on his face.

Something like relief.

As if he'd caught an egg just before it hit the floor.

I don't know what changed his mind. Perhaps the sight of Spud, trembling at my feet.

Or the look on my own face as I stood there waiting.

He glanced over his shoulder one last time.

And then I stepped back as he came through the door and took the porch steps in one leap, Spud at his heels, heedless of the rain.

I ran after them down the muddy lane. When I glanced back at the house, I saw his mother at the window—dark and faceless. His father at the mouth of the toolshed, a mallet in his hand.

Both of them looked bigger than they should.

And I felt smaller.

But I also felt a swell of freedom as I took off at speed after Andy and Spud, the house behind us growing smaller as we ran.

CHAPTER THIRTY-TWO

"Help me turn her on her side," Andy said when we reached Nora, who was still lying on the threshing floor.

Then he knelt next to her and gently lifted her head into his lap.

The dogs in their pens grew quiet as they watched.

"She'll be okay." Andy smoothed the hair from her face and made sure she was breathing all right. "We'll just let her wake up on her own."

With the flat of his hand, he made slow circles on her back, hushing softly when she began to groan.

This was an Andy I hadn't seen since the day he'd rescued the baby sparrows. And then buried the one he couldn't save.

"What's wrong with her?" I said.

"I'm not sure. I didn't see what started it."

"Neither did I. But she was twitching all over when I found her."

Andy glanced at me. "My grandmother used to get that way sometimes. And then she'd end up like this. My daddy called them fits. My grandma called them seizures. Either way, it was something to do with her brain."

And I remembered hearing that from my own grandma, who had grown up with Andy's.

I pictured the two of them as girls in braids and church frocks, swinging on tree swings, making up songs. "What did you do when it happened to your grandma?"

He kept his eyes on Nora. "My daddy doesn't hold much truck with doctors. When my grandma got like this, we'd help her through it. That's all."

"Nora was acting strange yesterday. She was talking, and then she suddenly got trembly, and I don't know . . ."

"What was she doing when that happened?"

I thought back. "She was talking about how her mother died."

Andy glanced at me. "And how did she die?"

"They were in a train wreck. Just a year ago. Nora tried to save her, but her mother died anyway."

Andy raised his eyebrows. "That one in Ohio?"

When I nodded, he said, "I read about it in the paper."

I wondered about him reading anything he didn't have to read.

"So the dogs in those pens are the ones I've been

hearing for weeks now," he said, too far away to see how beat up they were. "Is she breeding them?"

"No," I replied. And left it at that.

He gave me a look but then turned his attention back to Nora, watching her closely as she slowly tried to wake up.

And I watched him, how he stroked her hair, how gentle he was.

His own hair was an untidy cap, darkened by the rain. It was clear that he had cut it himself and mended his own clothes as well. I could see how he had repaired the knees of his work pants, the mismatched stitches wandering around the patches like bird tracks. How he had used bits of wire for boot laces.

And he was thin. Like Spud, too bony. But he looked strong overall. Tough from head to toe. But still too young for anything but a dusting of peach fuzz on his cheeks.

"I found your cow," I said, watching his face.

He turned to me, his eyes hardening a bit. "You found Honk?"

I nodded. "At the Turtle Stone. I put her in the barn with our cows."

It was interesting to watch him trying to sort that out, sort out what to say.

I decided to spare him. "You didn't want her to be butchered, so you hid her."

He scowled at me. "What do you know about it?"

I considered his hands. How chapped they were. His knuckles skinned and raw.

"Did you save me, too? When I was struck?"

But that was when Nora opened her eyes.

"It's all right now," Andy said as she tried to sit up. "Just lie still for another minute."

"Andy?" I said. "Did you hear me?"

"I don't know what you're talking about," he replied.

"I'm talking about—"

"Hush, now," he said softly, and I wasn't sure whether he was talking to me or Nora, who was staring at him, cringing like a feral cat. "Easy, now. Easy. You're all right now."

But she didn't relax until she saw me there, too, her eyes slowly coming into focus. "Annabelle?"

"It's okay, Nora." I took her hand. "You're okay."

She turned back to Andy. "Who are you?" Her voice was hoarse.

"Andy Woodberry," he said calmly. "From just down the road."

"I found you and ran to Andy's place to call the doctor," I said, "but his telephone's out. Same as yours. So he came to help."

"That's enough for now," Andy murmured to me. "She's going to be hazy for a while."

Nora took a long, careful breath and climbed slowly to her feet, wavering a bit.

Andy held on to her arm, and she let him, the two of them staggering over to a bale of hay where Andy sat her down.

He perched alongside her. "You just rest here for a while and then we'll get you home."

I remembered how scared Nora had seemed when Henry and I had first met her. She was more scared now, but not of Andy. That was clear from the way she grew calmer as he talked.

"That's your missing dog, come home," she said, staring at Spud.

"This is Spud." Andy reached down to knuckle him behind the ear. The dog trembled, his tail tucked between his legs. "He's a little nervous."

I reckoned the dogs in their pens were a worry to poor Spud, who had just recently been locked up in a cage alongside so many others, first at the pound and then at the animal hospital.

"He's nervous as a rule," Andy said, "but even nervouser since he got home."

Nora kept her eyes on Spud. "Why, as a rule?"

"I found him in a trash barrel, in Sewickley. Just a pup. Thrown out like an old shoe." He knelt down, and Spud put his nose into the crook of Andy's neck. "If he didn't start off nervous, I expect some time in a trash barrel when he was just born did the trick."

And I was amazed that he was telling this to a woman he'd just met, when he'd never said as much to me.

She glanced at Andy. "Why more nervous since he got home?"

Andy roughed up the fur along Spud's neck. "He was lost for two months. Been home for only a bit. I expect it'll take some time for him to believe all's well."

But I knew that a mother who slapped a boy for no reason at all was likely to kick a dog for much less. And from what I knew of Andy's father, I suspected he'd done some kicking of his own.

I saw no "all's well" in Spud's life. Or Andy's, either. But the best of it seemed to be right there with us, in that barn.

"Andy's like you," I told her. "He saved Spud here. And he saved an old cow from being butchered."

Even through her hazy exhaustion, Nora smiled a little. "My father rescued an old horse once, long past when it should have been pulling anyone's plow." She glanced up at us, her eyes tired. "I shouldn't admit to such a thing, but I guess I can trust a boy who steals a cow, which is just as bad. Or good, depending on how you look at it."

Andy glared at me fiercely. "And nobody's business, either way."

I didn't know what I'd done to deserve such a look, but I decided not to glare back, though it took some effort.

"You made it my business when you hid her on our farm."

He shook his head. "The Turtle Stone isn't yours."

I thought about that, while Nora watched us carefully. "No, it's not, though it's on our land."

I thought about the Turtle Stone. What it meant to me. What it had surely meant to other people, back and back to the beginning of things.

And I thought about what Andy and Betty had done there, sharpening the wire that had cut my brother James. Using the stone to do that.

How could the boy who'd done such a thing be the same boy who'd sheltered an old cow there? Who had risked another beating to help a sick woman he'd never met before?

"What's the Turtle Stone?" Nora said.

I noticed that her shoulders were sagging, her head low. "We'll show you when you're stronger."

Andy said, "We will?" With a slight emphasis on the "we."

He sounded annoyed.

"But for now let's get you to the house." I took one arm and gestured for Andy to take the other.

She pulled away. "I came out here to tend to the dogs. They need fresh water."

"We'll come back out to do that," Andy said.

I wanted to say, *We will?* But I left it alone.

It was enough, said once. Said at all.

CHAPTER THIRTY-THREE

We heard Mr. Edelman calling for Nora as we were settling her into bed. "And why is this mutt out here on the porch?" he hollered.

"He'll be mad at me," Nora mumbled.

Andy said, "You were supposed to be resting?"

She nodded. "We needed food. For the dogs. Else he wouldn't have left me alone."

I reckoned she had insisted he go. And I guessed that she was right about him being mad.

He was.

"She was in the barn?!" he said when we went down the stairs and told him what had happened. He glared at Andy. "You must be the Woodberry boy belongs to that white-eyed mutt."

I expected Andy to glare right back. Fight fire with fire. But he surprised me. "I'm Andy," he said mildly.

"Annabelle ran to our place to call the doctor, but our line's down, too. So I came."

Which calmed Mr. Edelman quite a bit. "Then I'm in your debt. But quiet's what Nora needs now, so I'll ask you to leave her to me."

"We told her we'd give the dogs some water." Andy turned for the door. "Food, too?"

But Mr. Edelman shook his head. "They've had breakfast. Won't need dinner for a while." He frowned at me. "What brought you here in the first place?"

I told him that Henry and I had decided to bring Buster back to finish healing. "But I suppose Nora has enough to do without another hurt dog."

"No, bring him down if you like. Nora's quite attached to that one. He'll do her good."

Andy waited for me by the door, and I could see the questions on his face. But when I heard Nora calling my name, I dashed back up the stairs to find her sitting on the edge of her bed, looking worried.

I rushed to her side. "What's wrong?"

"That boy. That Andy." She shook her head. "He's seen the dogs! And I never should have said anything about the horse my father took. Or anything else! I don't know what I was thinking."

"You weren't yourself, but don't worry. I'll make sure he understands. And I don't think he'd say a word about all that anyway." I gentled her back down into her bed. "He's not the nicest boy, but he's good to animals."

Which reminded me of what my grandma has said. About that very thing being the measure of a person.

Nora gazed up at me. "What you told us. At lunch. You said Andy was part of all that trouble with your friend Toby."

"That's true. He was."

"But you want me to trust him now? That same boy?"

"Except I think maybe he's not the same boy." I rubbed my face with my hand. "Or he is, only I didn't know him well enough."

But Nora had closed her eyes again, and I left her to her sleep.

Andy waited until we were on our way to the barn before he asked why we'd bring Buster back to the Edelmans' to heal.

"Nora's good with animals. She's helping the ones in the barn, but she doesn't want people to know about it."

"Then she'd better figure out how to shut them up."

He was right. They were a noisy bunch. But I didn't like his tone.

"You're always saying things are none of my business," I said. "Well, the dogs are Nora's business. So you can't tell anyone about them."

"Why not?"

"Because Nora doesn't deserve any more trouble than she's already had. And because she and her father rescue dogs that need rescuing. Patch them up, find better homes for them far from where they'd been."

He stared at me. "Like Spud."

"Like Spud, before you found him in that trash can," I replied. "Like Honk, but a bit smaller."

We walked on toward the barn through the last drizzly bits of rain.

As we reached the door, Andy said, "How did you know Buster was here?"

"I could hear him from the road," I said without thinking about it.

Andy stopped again. "You could tell his bark from the others?"

I looked for a long moment at his battered face. His angry eyes. The way he stood, poised for flight.

This was a boy I'd feared and loathed for such a long time.

But this was also a boy who had rescued a puppy, saved a cow from the butcher, treated Nora as if she'd been made of glass.

Even though he might easily have done otherwise.

So I told him the story. All of it.

"It's gone now," I said, Andy's eyes on my face. "The way I could feel things. The way I saw things and heard things—every sense, really, so sharp—all that has gone back to what it used to be. Except I'm extra aware now of things I knew before but maybe didn't quite know." I paused. "I notice more now."

As I once had. Before Toby's death. Before I'd begun to doubt myself.

Andy took a long, thoughtful moment to digest what I'd said, gazing off into the trees, absently rubbing Spud's head. "Sounds like a tall tale to me."

I sighed. "That's what the doctors in Pittsburgh thought. They said they needed evidence. But the doctor at the animal hospital believed me when I told him what was ailing the dogs there. Including Spud."

Andy looked up sharply. "And what was that?"

I looked at my boots. "He was lonely."

Andy went still for a moment and then knelt down and put his head against Spud's, and the two of them were like one creature for a while.

"Do *you* believe me?" I said.

Andy stood up. "Does it matter?"

Well, it did, I thought. Though it didn't.

"Let's go look after those dogs," I said.

CHAPTER THIRTY-FOUR

Andy and I spent some time with the dogs, giving them fresh water and learning whatever they decided to teach us.

Turned out, Andy learned quite a lot.

He didn't know exactly what had happened to them (though, to be fair, I hadn't known the details myself), but he got the most important part: that they'd been hurt.

I realized he knew more about that than I did. About being hurt. Though he also knew more about the other side of that coin, too.

I watched him as he lugged a bucket of cistern water across the threshing floor, Spud following close behind.

And I decided I had waited long enough.

"How could you rig that wire across the path?" I said.

He stopped so suddenly that the water sloshed over the rim of the bucket.

"What wire?" He scowled at me.

"The one that cut my brother." Though of course he knew. He had to know.

He went on to the last of the pens where Zeus waited, and I decided I wouldn't say anything about Mr. Graf or the reward he was offering.

When Andy went into the pen, the dog backed into a far corner. I could no longer feel the menace that I'd felt before, but even from where I stood, I could hear the rumble in his throat.

"The wire you and Betty strung across the path," I said, my eyes on the dog. "The one meant for me."

But I put all that aside when the big bull suddenly lowered his head and began to creep slowly toward Andy, who was busy filling the dog's dish, his eyes on his work. "Andy, come out of there," I said urgently.

"Why? So you can yell at me?" But then he straightened up and saw the bull approaching and went still. "Annabelle, I know that dog," he said, edging away.

I pulled open the gate, and he backed out quickly, latching it behind him.

I let go of the breath I'd been holding.

"I know that dog," he said again.

"Did Mr. Graf come to your farm?" I asked.

"Who?" Andy said, and I could see that he was confused.

"Never mind. Just tell me how you know that dog."

He glanced at me and then back at the bull, clearly nervous. "I shouldn't tell you."

"Then don't," I said impatiently. "Tell me about the wire."

But with Zeus just on the other side of the gate, his eyes fixed on us both, Andy told me about him instead. "My father took me a couple of times to a place in Aliquippa where there's a pit."

I imagined a hole in the ground, like the ones that had given Wolf Hollow its name. Ditches where people had trapped wolves and killed them for the bounty. "A pit? What for?"

"A *pit*," he said. "For dog fights."

I didn't understand, though Nora had said something similar. "Why would anyone want dogs to fight?"

He looked away and muttered his answer.

I didn't catch all of it. "So people can *what*?"

"So people can bet on them!" he blurted.

I felt cold suddenly. "On which one will win?"

Andy nodded, but he still wouldn't look at me.

"And how does a dog win a fight like that?"

"One dog lives. The other dies."

I wondered how anyone could be mean enough to profit from a dog's death. But I knew that anyone could be anything. All they had to do was decide. "So the bull in that pen there . . . ?"

Andy glanced at the terrier. "He won the last fight I was at. He killed the other dog."

I remembered when I'd first seen Zeus. The darkness I'd felt in him.

I stared at Andy. "Did you bet on him?"

"Of course not! I never went near the pit. My father tried to make me. He . . . he *laughed* at me when I wanted to wait in the truck. And then he made me go with him into the barn where they had the pit." He looked pale, hollow-eyed. "I didn't watch the fight, but I heard it. And I saw that dog afterward, after he won."

I thought back. "You said a couple of fights. That your father took you to *a couple* of those fights," I said. "You went back? Even after you knew what it would be like, you went back?"

Andy shook his head. "I didn't know where we were going. I wouldn't have gone back if I'd known. And I couldn't run off."

"You ran off and hid in our potato house when *you* were the one who got beat up."

"I didn't hide!" he snapped. "And I got in trouble in the first place because I saved Honk." For a moment, he looked at me the way Spud looked at him. But then he said, "I don't know why I'm wasting my breath."

"And I don't know what to believe." It was true. I

didn't. There seemed to be several versions of Andy, and I didn't know which of them was the truth.

I felt like a cyclone walking, my mind filled with ruckus and spin.

"Believe what you want," he said bitterly.

We were both quiet for a long moment, Spud leaning against Andy's leg, the other dogs making small noises in their pens, the rock doves cooing and gurgling in the rafters.

"My father said I shouldn't go near you again," I said slowly.

Andy crossed his arms. His eyes went flat.

I looked steadily back at him. "He reckoned I'd remind you of the things you've done, though I don't know why you'd need a reminder. How could you forget any of that?"

He looked away again. "Who says I did?"

The silence between us stretched out like a slingshot.

And then he left, Spud at his heels.

For a long moment, I stood listening to the come-and-go cawing of distant crows. The lowing of cows. Quite aware of how very much I didn't understand.

I turned again to the bull terrier.

He stared at me.

"You must think it's crazy," I said. "The things people do."

Nora seemed to think the same thing.

I knew they weren't wrong. But I didn't want my heart to be that hard.

I watched the terrier as he stood there, so still he might have been a museum dog, carved from stone.

My grandfather had said of Andy, "You get what you give." So far, I'd given Zeus no reason to bite me. If he was leery of all people, on principle, that might not matter.

But it might.

When I opened the gate, the big bull backed away again.

I didn't look straight at him, which was something I'd learned from the farm dogs I'd known, each pack ruled by one boss dog who was patient with those that crouched low or rolled over, risking their soft underbellies, but punished those who looked him in the eye.

When I glanced at him from under my brows, I saw Zeus staring at me, his face serious.

I looked away again, closing the gate behind me.

Then I slowly, carefully lowered myself to the straw until I was sitting with my back against the fence, my knees up in front of me, some small protection if things went wrong.

And I put my head down so my face rested on my knees, my arms tucked in against my chest: a small, face-less, ordinary lump of a person.

The hair on my neck stood up as I realized that we were

alone inside a cage of sorts, perhaps like the one where he'd killed other dogs.

No one was telling us to fight. We had no reason to fight. We had nothing to gain by fighting. But I reckoned that some things, once learned, were hard to unlearn.

"Hello, old son," I said slowly. Something I'd heard my grandpap say to dogs he'd known. "This is no pit. And no one's betting on either one of us."

I made sure to speak in the same singsongy voice my mother used around the feral cats that had their kittens in our barn every spring.

It calmed me. I hoped it calmed Zeus.

When I peeked up over my knees, I saw him take a step toward me, blinking and yawning away his nerves, his head down, no wag at all in his tail.

"Come on, now." I lowered my face again. "I won't hurt you. And you have no reason to hurt me, though I know people have been mean to you."

I felt him coming closer. Heard him. Felt the heat of him as he drew near.

I didn't move. Not one muscle.

I wondered if he could sense my fear.

So I let myself imagine the feel of his soft jowl against my hand. Let myself imagine a peaceful look in his eye. And didn't startle when he put his muzzle against the top of my bowed head and took a good, long sniff.

CHAPTER THIRTY-FIVE

"*That's a bad idea,*" Andy whispered from beyond the gate when he came back to find me sitting in the pen, the bull lying with his head in my lap so I could scratch behind his ears.

The dog lifted his head with a sigh. I kept my eyes down as he climbed to his feet and put some distance between us. Then I carefully stood up, all my movements smooth and slow. We both stretched and yawned for a moment before I gently let myself out of the pen.

Andy shook his head, Spud trembling by his side. "That dog could have ripped you to bits."

"But he didn't," I said.

"But he could have."

"But he didn't."

Andy sighed. "It's like talking to a parakeet."

"He had no reason to rip me to bits."

"Since when do people needs reasons for what they do?"

I huffed at that. "Mudpie's not a person."

"Mudpie?"

"He used to be called Zeus, but I'm working on a new name. Mudpie, maybe."

Andy's eyebrows went up. "How do you know he was called Zeus?"

I paused for a moment to think again about the trust Nora had placed in me . . . and whether I could risk trusting Andy.

"He belongs to a man named Mr. Graf."

"That man you mentioned before?"

"I thought maybe that was how why you recognized the bull. Mr. Graf's been driving around all over the place, looking for him." *In for a penny, in for a pound*, I thought. "He's even offered a reward. Ten dollars."

Andy whistled softly. "That's a lot of money."

"But, Andy, you can't—"

"Relax," he said, scowling. "I wouldn't turn that dog in for a *million* dollars. Not to that man. He's a devil."

I thought back to Mr. Graf's perfect smile. His lovely green eyes. "Are you sure it's the same man? The Mr. Graf I met looked very nice."

"He *looked* nice? That's how you decide about a person?"

He wasn't wrong. Betty and Toby had both taught me

not to count on what someone looked like, and I should have known better, but I wasn't about to be schooled by Andy Woodberry. "You thought Toby was a villain because of how *he* looked."

"Because of how he *acted*," Andy said. "Because he rambled all over the place with those guns of his and never said a word to anyone."

"He said plenty to me."

"Well, good for you, Annabelle. But we're not talking about Toby. We're talking about Mr. Graf. Who dragged a rottweiler out of the pit by one leg and threw him on a garbage heap for burning. I saw him do it. And it makes no difference at all what he was wearing or how pretty he was when he did it."

I could picture such a thing, though I wished I couldn't. "I didn't know that, Andy."

"Well, you don't know everything."

"No. I don't. And neither do you."

We spent a moment staring at each other.

"I hoped someone else was to blame for those awful cuts on Mudpie's face," I finally admitted. "But I believe what you said about Mr. Graf. So we'll keep Mudpie here and treat him right, and maybe he'll come around."

Andy shook his head. "Mudpie's a stupid name."

"It's better than Zeus."

"But *Mudpie*?"

"You named a cow Honk."

"Which is why I came back. Because of her." He said it firmly, as if it were important to get that straight.

I made sure there was no grit in my voice when I said, "What about her?"

He sighed. "I can't go home yet, not after you came over and made such a mess of everything, so I reckoned I could go see her. Maybe stay with her tonight."

From potato house to cow barn.

I shrugged. "She's your cow."

"But it's your barn."

"Then yes, if it's okay with my father."

He nodded. "But you'll do the asking?"

I said I would. "As soon as I get home."

I turned to go.

At the barn door, I looked back to find Andy still standing by Mudpie's pen.

"Are you coming?" I said, puzzled.

Andy walked slowly across the threshing floor to join me. "I thought maybe I should wait until you asked him."

"Oh, he'll say yes," I said. "I know he will."

CHAPTER THIRTY-SIX

As we walked down the Edelmans' lane to the road, Spud trotting along beside us, I said, "Why did you leave Honk at the Turtle Stone?"

"Because she wouldn't fit under my bed," he replied, but without much ire.

We walked on for a bit. The rain had stopped, but the whole world was still sopping wet, steaming lazily in the sun that broke through the clouds in bright patches across the flat land.

"You could have asked me," I said. "I would have taken her to our barn straightaway, without days on her own in between."

"She didn't mind. I went to see her morning and night, took her fresh hay, made sure she had water, milked her if she needed it."

"And kept her from being butchered. But surely lots of your cows have gone that way over the years."

He gave me his customary glare, plucking at the saplings that grew up alongside the road. "Plenty," he said.

We cut down through the long rows of field corn that grew between the road and Wheeler's Run. The stalks were already up past our waists though it was only June, and I was eager for when they were taller even than my father, when walking down the rows was like being in a secret. Invisible to everything except the occasional birds weaving their threads of color in the blue cap of sky overhead.

We slogged across the muddy ground through all that green promise and hopped the rocks that spanned the run where it was shallow enough to wet nothing but our boots if we slipped, Spud splashing along happily, distracted by crayfish and tree-shadow, stopping for a long cool drink while we waited on the far bank.

I felt quite calm about being with Andy, despite all the ups and downs of our day so far, of our lives so far. But as we took a path through the woods, I pictured him with Betty instead, walking that same path, under those same trees. And I felt torn once again, right down the middle, as if I were two girls, and I realized that I wanted more than anything else to feel like one whole person again.

Perhaps that was coming. But for now, as before, as always, there was work to be done.

When the path merged with the one that led up from the schoolhouse to our orchards, I went on just a bit more to where my brother James had been hurt by the wire strung between the trees.

There, I stopped.

"Do you know where we are?" I asked.

Andy frowned at me. "Don't you?"

I stepped off the path to finger the place where the wire had left a scar on the tree.

Andy shook his head, backing away. "Annabelle, not that again."

"Why not?" I said.

"Because it's finished and done with." He sighed. "And because I didn't do that."

"You didn't help Betty sharpen that wire on the Turtle Stone?"

He held up his hands. "I did that part, but she never told me what she meant to do with it. I swear."

"Well, what did you think it was for, Andy?"

Andy looked into the trees. "Nothing good. But not that."

I tried to imagine a different use for a sharp wire, but I couldn't think of one.

"And when she put that wire in Toby's shack, to make it look like he'd done such a thing, why didn't you speak up?"

Andy stared at his boots. "I didn't know about all that until it was too late."

"You knew she was trying to hurt him."

He nodded. "But I didn't know what kind of hurt. And I've already told you—I didn't know Toby like you did, Annabelle. The whole thing was like a runaway horse."

Which I understood. I understood about things whirling out of control. "But you waited all this time to say so?"

"It doesn't feel like *all this time*. I still feel like I'm on that horse." He heaved a sigh. "Everything's still a blur."

"Well, it's not clear to me, either. It's terrifying, how things just happen without people knowing why."

He made an impatient sound. "That's the way things are."

Which was as awful as anything else he'd said.

"So Betty could just decide to beat me? And not have to answer to anyone?"

"She beat you?" Andy exclaimed, his eyes wide. "Until this minute, I didn't know she did that, Annabelle. I didn't know anything about that, I swear. She just liked to make mischief, and things got out of hand."

I was almost sorry I'd started this. Every word of it made me want to run home and hide in the barn with a book and an apple and let the world go on without me. I let out a long breath. "You can make up all the excuses you want, Andy, but they don't matter."

"Then what does?" he said, his voice hoarse.

"Plenty." And I heard the echo. Andy using that same word to talk about the steady stream of cows that had outlived their usefulness and been sent off to their gloomy deaths.

But it also meant what I had. Had always had. Plenty.

Anything could mean anything.

I started again up the path. "You want to be done with all this. Well, so do I. But there's one more thing you should see."

I climbed past the wheat field toward the spot where I'd been struck in the storm but then walked a few steps farther to the east, Andy and Spud following behind.

When we reached Toby's grave, I stopped, and the three of us stood quietly, a breeze skimming across the top of the hill and out across Wolf Hollow.

I imagined deer in the woods below, lifting their heads as our scent reached them.

I'd once asked my grandfather why a deer was brown all over except for the white under-tail it flashed when it ran.

"It waves that white flag to draw a predator's eye," he

had said. "To draw him toward where she just was and not to where she's headed."

I wondered why that memory had risen just now, there at Toby's grave, with Andy nearby.

I looked at him standing in the sunlight, the tips of his hair riffling in the breeze like feathers.

He seemed confused. Like he had something to say but wasn't sure what it was.

A honeybee drifted past my ear, purring, harmless.

"You ought to spend some time here," I said. "You ought to tell Toby that you wish you could take it all back, what you and Betty did."

After a long moment, Andy said, "I can't."

"Can't what? Can't tell him? Or can't take it back?"

"Just *can't*, Annabelle." He sounded tired. "Besides, what difference would it make? He's dead. And I wasn't the one who killed him."

The look he gave me was hard to read. But whatever else was in Andy's eyes, there was anger, too.

"Why are you looking at me like that?" I said.

"Like what?"

"Like you're angry with me."

"Because I am!"

"You're angry with *me*?"

"You act like you've never made a mistake," he said, his voice hard. "You expect people to be perfect."

"That's not true!" I sputtered. "I've made plenty of mistakes. And I don't expect people to be perfect. But I do think they should know why they do what they do."

He opened his mouth. Shut it again. Scrubbed his face with his hands and made a noise as if he were strangling. "All at once? I'm supposed to know that all at once?" He shook his head. "That's not possible. Not for me it's not."

Or for me, either, I realized. All through the troubles with Toby, all through the long winter that followed, all through my saddest spring, all through the days since the lightning strike, I'd been trying to find my way.

And I was still trying.

"Then a little at a time," I said. "Which, you're right, is the way it happens. Is the way it happens for me, too."

CHAPTER THIRTY-SEVEN

I left Andy and Spud outside the barn while I went in to find my father and my grandpap and the boys at their chores.

They were all gathered around the corn sheller, Buster laid out nearby on a bale of hay.

I waved at my father to turn off the noisy sheller.

"Would it be all right if Andy stayed in the barn with Honk for the night?" I asked.

He looked puzzled about that. "Why doesn't he just take her on home, now that she's found?"

But the answer wasn't mine to tell. "It's complicated," I said.

After a moment, my father nodded. "Then sure. If he wants to stay for the night, I don't see why not."

Henry made a sound in his throat. "*I* do."

My father frowned at him. "You do what?"

"I do see why not," Henry said. "He shouldn't be here at all."

"When you're the one farming this land, you can be the one who decides things," my father said, his voice stern.

"What about me?" James said.

My father said, "What about you?"

"When do I get to decide things?"

"Right now," my father said. "You can decide to help your grandpap with that corn."

James sighed and turned back to the sheller.

"You too," my father said to Henry, who looked downcast until I said, "We'll take Buster back to . . . Mr. Edelman tomorrow. He said it would be fine. And you can go down there whenever you want, Henry."

Which made him stand up taller. "But I'll make sure my chores are done first," he told my father.

"I know you will. Now get on with that corn." My father waited while I fetched Andy and Spud, and then we headed for the lower barn, down the stairs and along a broad corridor with a dirt floor and a low ceiling. Gates at each end opened onto pastureland, the stalls for the horses and cows lined up along one side. The smell of the animals was strong here, swallows swooping in to pour themselves into the cups of their nests in the rafters overhead.

We stopped outside Daisy's stall. "Honk's out in the

pasture with the others," my father said. "But she'll sleep in here. And you can certainly stay here as well, Andy." He hesitated. "But wouldn't you rather take her home? To show your father she's been found?"

I imagined he saw that as a way to patch things up between them.

"Except she wasn't lost," Andy said with a sigh. "I took her so she wouldn't be butchered." He looked at the ground, his hands in his pockets.

"I see." My father rubbed his jaw with the flat of his hand. "Well, there's room here for you and Honk both."

"And Spud, too." I nodded at a bale of straw. "You can lay down some of that fresh for a bed. I'll bring you a blanket."

"I don't need one," he replied.

"Of course you do," my father said. "And you can leave Honk here for good, if you want. As long as you pay me for her feed."

Andy looked up. "If my father finds out she's here, he'll want her back. For the meat."

We'd all lived for years with war rations. We all knew the value of beef.

But we also knew the value of the calves Honk had given up. The milk that had been meant for those calves. The years she still had left, which ought to be hers.

My father met my eye. Chewed his lip. "I can try to pay him something for her, over time, if you'll work it off,

Andy. That and what her feed costs. And if you'll muck out her stall. Is she worth that much to you?"

Andy's face was a puzzle. "Yes. That will be all right."

Though I wondered how he'd manage to spend time working here, working at home, going to school when the time came, at least some of the time. All that and more.

And I wondered how it would be to have Andy spending time here, in the places where I'd always felt safest.

I considered him as he stood there alongside my father, in a barn I'd loved all my life.

I looked at his ragged hair. The state of his old clothes.

And his hands. Most of all, I looked at his hands.

"*Andy saved my life*," I whispered, suddenly quite sure that it was true.

"He did what?" my father said, leaning closer.

"He saved my life," I said in a stronger voice.

The expression on Andy's face convinced me that I was right.

For the first time in a long while, Andy looked like a kid. Like a boy still some distance from being a man. His eyes softer than I'd ever seen them.

And I felt softer, too. But stronger as well. As if I'd been given fresh soil, enough water, and plenty of sun to sprout new growth, climb upward, and bloom.

A seed has a shell for a reason, I realized. But that shell needs to open.

I had no interest in being locked away. Not any part of me.

As I watched my father understand what I'd said, it was easy to know how soft he, too, felt in that moment.

I watched as his eyes opened wide and then closed altogether. He stood like that for a moment, trembling a little, and then opened them again.

"Is that true? Did you save her life?"

Andy nodded reluctantly.

We waited.

My father cleared his throat. "I'm going to need more than a nod."

"Then, yes," Andy said. He looked annoyed. "I'd been with Honk at the Turtle Stone, and I saw Annabelle through the trees, on the path coming up from the schoolhouse. Just before the storm broke." He swallowed hard. "It came on so fast, I figured she was sure to be caught. So I ran along to see if, well . . . to see." He stopped. "It was terrible, the way it knocked her flat and how—" He stopped again to swallow hard. "There was smoke coming off her arm."

My father made a sound in his throat and then took a long breath. "How did you know what to do?"

"You mean when she wasn't breathing?"

My father closed his eyes again for a moment. "Did someone teach you how to start her heart again?"

"No. It just seemed like the thing to do." Andy glanced

at my face. "I didn't want to leave you there, but I saw your daddy coming, and I knew you'd be all right."

Once again, I felt that rough hand on my cheek, and I knew that I had seen more in that moment—when I'd been unable to see—than in all the months before and since.

"But why didn't you stay?" I asked him. "Why did you run off when you saw my father coming? And why didn't you tell me when I asked you before?"

In that moment, Andy no longer looked much like a boy.

To my father, he said, "I'm obliged for a place to sleep, but I'll just be here for the one night, to get Honk settled, though I'll come back every morning to work off the debt, if that's all right."

My father shook his head and cleared his throat again. "You don't owe me anything. We'll look after Honk. There's no debt to work off."

At the expression on Andy's face, my father said, struggling a bit with his voice, "You saved Annabelle's life, Andy. I'm glad to help you save Honk's. It's the least I can do."

We stood in silence for a moment, Spud snapping at a fly.

I nodded at the straw again. "I'll bring that blanket. And you'll need a pillow, too. But supper before that. I'll ring the bell when it's time to come in."

And I barely made it out of the barn before I began to cry.

CHAPTER THIRTY-EIGHT

"Annabelle! What's wrong!" my grandmother exclaimed when I stumbled through the mudroom, shedding my boots and rain gear helter-skelter, and found her with my mother at the kitchen table, writing letters.

"I don't know!" I sobbed, dropping into a chair alongside them and putting my head in my arms.

"What do you mean, you don't know?" my mother said. "Are you hurt?"

"No, not hurt." I sat up and wiped my face. "I'm just so sad and confused and frustrated, and I think I've been too mean to Andy."

I saw the two of them exchange a look.

"This is about *Andy*?" my mother said.

"Yes, but in about a thousand different ways."

My grandmother took my hand in hers and said, in a gentle voice, "Then why don't you tell us about one of those thousand things."

So I told them how Andy had made excuses for what Betty had done.

"He said he didn't know that she'd hurt me, and he didn't think she'd done the rest of it on purpose, but of course she did, anyone could see that, and he was with her so much I don't know how he could think otherwise, unless that's what he *wanted* to think—"

"Annabelle!" my mother said. "Slow down now. You're all worked up."

"I know! And I don't want to be worked up. I want to understand everything a lot better than I do. I want to know what's true and what's not. And how to tell the difference. But most of all—" And here I stopped and took a deep breath and let it out again. "I want to know how to feel about a boy who has done some terrible things, even if he's not as bad as I thought he was—and he saved a dog, and then a cow, and then . . . me."

That brought everything to a halt.

"He saved you?" my grandma said. "How?"

"*Was he the one who found you after the lightning strike?*" my mother whispered.

I nodded.

"And you want to know if that balances the scales?" My grandma sighed.

I nodded again. "I feel guilty when I think about letting all the rest of it go just because he started my heart again."

"*Just because he . . .*" My mother let out a little gasp. "Annabelle, there is no *just* about that."

My grandmother looked at me, her face lovely and sad. "But there is forgiveness, my girl. A good deed doesn't erase a bad one, but it's worth a lot. And I happen to think it's worth even more, considering . . . well, considering it's Andy we're talking about."

I rubbed my eyes. "You mean it takes a lot of gumption for a bully to do something nice?"

"I guess you could call it gumption." She waggled her head. "Although I liked what you said before—about what's waiting below the surface to be woken up."

"And you think I ought to forgive him for what he did with Betty?"

"That's entirely up to you. But whatever you decide, make it your own decision. No one else's."

I thought about everything as I helped put supper on the table: sliced beets we'd canned the year before, mashed sweet potatoes with butter and cracked pepper, hot buns stuffed with roasted carrots, and thick, crusty slices of applewood bacon.

I thought about it as I poured cold milk, hot coffee, lemonade for my grandma.

I thought about it as I went out to ring the bell.

And I thought about it as Aunt Lily came out of her

bedroom, declaring herself famished and parched and beyond exhausted. As the boys came in from the barn, shedding their boots, washing up their grubby hands, Andy standing back a bit, silent, watching it all with a look of puzzlement on his face, his eyes widening when he saw the table. All the food laid out in dishes. As my father pulled out a chair for him. As he sat.

And I thought about it as we said grace and began to pass the dishes around, Aunt Lily wondering who in the world had thought to pair roasted carrots and bacon in a *sandwich*, though she practically hummed when she took a bite, and the boys quibbled about whether Superman was more powerful than the Green Hornet, my grandma gently reminding James to use his napkin, not his sleeve, my mother hopping up from time to time to pour more coffee, more milk, my father quiet, like my grandpap, while I watched it all, too, and Andy as well.

"*Is it always like this?*" he whispered to me, his plate as clean as it had ever been.

"You mean supper?" Had I not been paying so much attention, I might have been confused by the question. "Yes. It's always like this."

"I never knew."

And I wasn't confused about that, either. "Do you want another sandwich?"

He stared at me. "Another?"

So I got up from the table and made it for him, put it on his plate, poured him some more milk, and passed him the rest, one dish at a time, until he had more of everything. "But save room for dessert. My mother made a strawberry pie with whipped cream."

He ate it all in silence, listening to the chatter, watching how my father leaned back in his chair and sighed with contentment, his eyes tired but not weary. How my mother stood behind him, resting her hands on his shoulders, and answered a question from my grandma, something about a quilting bee at the church, before she began to clear the plates, telling Andy to keep his fork, passing the pie in perfect wedges so red, so white with cream, they were almost too pretty to eat.

"Did you tell the boys?" I asked my father, and everyone got quiet.

"Tell us what?" Henry looked from me to Andy and back again.

"Does Annabelle have another superpower?" James said, his mouth full of pie.

"No," my father said, "but Andy does."

And he told them how Andy had found me after the lightning strike and brought me back to life.

My mother and grandma had already heard the story, but they listened intently as they heard it again, and the others, hearing it for the first time, sat quiet and still in their chairs.

James, who had plenty of reason to be angry with Andy, had never seemed to hold a grudge, though the scar on his forehead was a constant reminder of what had happened the year before. As he listened, he began to smile at Andy, his eyes round.

My grandpap had plenty of reason to be angry with Andy, too, though his was a matter of what a person should be, how a person should behave. *Should* was behind how he felt, now and in most things. What Andy should be. And what he shouldn't, for that matter.

But as my grandpap listened to my father tell the story, he nodded and smiled, as if to say, *There. That's better.*

Henry was different. Henry had seen my troubles and come to be a bit fierce about defending me, though he was younger, with fears and worries of his own.

As he listened to this news about Andy, he seemed doubtful, looking for the lie. But when Andy said, "There was no one there but me. I didn't really have any choice," Henry leaned back in his chair, quiet and thoughtful. Perhaps he was thinking, as I was, about what other choice Andy might have made, and why he hadn't.

"My daddy likes to sit on the front porch with my grandpap after supper," I told Andy. "You can go out there with them if you want. And I'll take you to the barn when I'm done redding up the kitchen."

But he said no, he'd stay where he was, and he did, sitting at the table while the boys went out to check on Buster in his wagon and chase rabbits from my mother's flower bed.

I told Andy to let Spud into the mudroom, that my mother wouldn't mind if we gave him a slice of bacon, a saucer of milk when no one was looking. Though Aunt Lily caught us and screeched for a while about a dog eating from a bowl meant for people, at which Andy actually smiled.

I was amazed that it was Aunt Lily who had finally accomplished such a feat, though to him she must have seemed comical, and we all must have seemed funny in the way we ignored her, as if she were a parrot in a cage, clever enough to squawk some English but not worth answering.

I remembered how Andy had called me a parakeet, and I vowed that I had come as close to being an Aunt Lily as I ever would.

"I don't think I've eaten so much in my whole life," Andy said as I took him out to the barn with a pillow and some blankets.

"Come in as soon as you're up in the morning, for breakfast. My mother will have something ready by five, so don't be shy about it."

He paused, glancing at me. "Will you be up by then?"

"Probably not."

"Then call me when you're up."

I figured he didn't want to sit alone in that kitchen with my parents. I could understand that.

"Where are you going?" he said when, instead of heading straight into the lower barn, I went around toward the upper part and the big doors that led onto the threshing floor.

"You don't really want to sleep with Honk and Daisy, do you?" I walked in and across the enormous room to the ladder that led to the hayloft.

He glanced up. "I wouldn't mind the loft instead."

Spud sat down alongside Andy's boot and sighed happily, his belly full of bacon.

"You can take him up, too," I said.

But when Andy turned for the ladder, I stopped him. "That loft is where Toby stayed, when it wasn't safe for him to be in his own place last year." I waited, watching his face. "When Betty told everyone he was a villain."

Andy met my eye this time. "But you're letting me stay there anyway?"

I nodded. "I'm trying to mean what I said at Toby's

grave. About letting go of all that and starting again. But I just can't understand why any of it was necessary."

"All that stuff we did?" I was pleased by the "we." That he wasn't making excuses anymore. I watched as his face settled, his eyes closed, and he gave himself up to an answer I hadn't expected. "I don't know why, either."

I wasn't happy with that, but it felt like the truth.

I handed him the bedding. "Good night."

He took it, his face curious. "James seems to think you still have superpowers."

I shrugged. "I haven't told them yet. Just Henry."

"Why not the others?"

I paused. "I'm not sure. I suppose I didn't want to disappoint them."

He laughed at that. "Because now you're just as ordinary as the rest of us?"

I felt my face turn pink. "You make me sound awful."

He shifted the bedding in his arms. "You're not awful." He turned for the ladder.

And I replayed those words as I watched him climb up the ladder one-handed, Spud under his arm, the bedding draped over his shoulder, and disappear into the shadows.

CHAPTER THIRTY-NINE

I got up the next morning, thinking about Andy—all the versions of him—which made me feel like I was more than one person, too.

So I decided to get on with my day and take things as they came, one bit at a time, before I whirled myself into even more confusion, like water down a drain.

When I made my way to the kitchen, I found the others at the table, but no Andy.

"I told him he was welcome to flapjacks," my mother said, "but he insisted on waiting for you." She raised her eyebrows. "He's been sitting out back for an hour."

James peered at me, a pillow of flapjack poised on his fork. "Is Andy your boyfriend now?"

Aunt Lily answered him with a swat of her hand and a quick "Hush up, boy. She's far too young for that sort of thing."

And down the drain I went.

"I don't know what he is," I muttered as I went to fetch him.

Andy was sitting on the porch steps, scratching Spud behind the ears. They both looked up when I opened the screen door. "If you want breakfast, you'd better get in here," I snapped.

"Good morning to you, too," Andy said, unfazed.

"You have hay in your hair," I said, resisting the urge to pick it out.

"And you have a bee in your bonnet, though I don't know why."

Which made two of us.

He sat down in the seat he'd had the night before, already part of the picture, and ate six flapjacks with butter and maple syrup before I'd finished my first.

My mother watched him thoughtfully, her feeding instinct on full alert. "Would you like some more?" she asked, reaching for the batter.

"No, thank you, ma'am." He pushed back his chair. "I'm late already."

"For what?" Henry said, not quite as gruff as he'd been the day before. I reckoned it was hard to stay angry with someone who'd eaten at your table, slept in your barn. Saved your sister's life.

"Work, same as you," Andy said.

My father laid down his fork. "We'll take you home directly. We're headed down there anyway, since Henry wants to take Buster back to Mr. Edelman."

"I thought Nora was the one helping Buster," Andy said.

Aunt Lily frowned. "Who's Nora?"

Andy looked at me sharply, and I realized I'd told him to keep the dogs a secret. I'd said nothing about Nora wanting to be left alone.

"Annabelle!" Henry said.

"I know! I'm sorry!"

"What?" Andy said, clearly confused. "Don't they know about Nora?"

"They do now," Henry said.

"Not really." My mother looked at us forbiddingly. "Though you three are about to tell us."

"She's Mr. Edelman's daughter." I sighed. "She's a . . ." I didn't want to say hermit, since it brought to mind the idea of an old man with a long beard in a cave. But I didn't know another word to describe someone who wanted to go away somewhere and be alone. "She doesn't like to be around people. She doesn't want them bothering her."

And then the dam broke and the whole story spilled out: how her mother had died, how she herself was sick, how her father had brought her to the countryside. And, finally, the dogs.

"You can see why she didn't want us to say anything,"

I said. "She just wants to be left alone. And that Mr. Graf who came here looking for his bull terrier . . . imagine what he'd do if he knew Zeus was with the Edelmans."

"Why in the world would you keep such secrets, Annabelle?" my father said, his voice rising.

I knew he was thinking about the mistakes I'd made before, trying to handle things bigger than my two hands could hold.

"If Annabelle's in trouble, so am I," Henry said.

"I am, too," Andy said carefully, as if he were feeling his way.

My father rolled his eyes. "Anyone else?"

"It wasn't my place to tell Nora's secret," I said. "And I would have told you about Zeus, except Mr. Graf shouldn't have him back."

"And why is that? Because your mother didn't like the look of him? That's hardly a good reason to—"

"No, Daddy. Because Zeus was all torn up when Mr. Edelman found him. And Andy said he's from a dog pit in Aliquippa."

"But I didn't go there on purpose," Andy said in a rush. "My father made me go, and I stayed as far from the pit as I could."

"What's a dog pit?" James asked.

"It's where dogs fight," Andy explained, "and people bet on which dog will kill the other one."

I wouldn't have explained it that way. Not to James. But it was clear that Andy hadn't said it to be mean. He had said it as a matter of fact. Like "there's a sun in the sky" or "summer follows spring."

But when he saw the reaction of the others around the table, he sighed. "I'm sorry."

Henry looked sick. They all did. Even Aunt Lily.

"And this . . . this Zeus is at the Edelmans'?" my father said, his face grim.

Aunt Lily shook her head. "Nothing good about that, any way you look at it."

"But how is that any different from Andy taking Honk, who's out there in our barn right now?" I said. "Or Spud, who'd been dumped in a trash can?"

"Honk is already Andy's cow," my grandpap said. "And whoever threw Spud away didn't care where he ended up."

"Mr. Graf threw away that terrier, too," I argued. "Worse than that."

I expected Aunt Lily to say something about beasts of burden or laws of the land, but she didn't . . . though my father did. "Unfortunately, there's no law against dog fights. Not in Pennsylvania anyway."

"Even so, we can't tell anyone else about Nora," I insisted, "or the dogs."

"Why are you looking at me?" Aunt Lily protested. "I am not now, nor have I ever been, a gossip, young lady."

Which was true. Whatever else she was, Aunt Lily was no tattletale.

"Do you all promise?" I looked at James.

"Scout's honor." He sketched an X across his chest with one finger.

"And if Mr. Graf comes back again?" my mother asked. "Looking for his dog?"

"It's not a lie to say nothing," Henry said.

"Well, but it is," my grandpap replied. "It's a lie of omission."

My father held up his hands. "All right." He looked hard at me. "You've learned a few things about doing the wrong thing for the right reason, and how that doesn't always work out the way you hope it will. But in this case, with those animals treated like they were—" He dropped his hands in his lap. "I won't decide for your mother or anyone else, but I'll keep quiet about them. That sits right with me."

"Me too," my mother said, "though I don't know how I'm going to stop myself from going to see that Nora of yours."

I'd figured as much. "I think you'd like her."

"Then let me know if she decides to let her fences down."

"And until then we'll keep our distance." My father stood up. "Now, I've got peaches to thin, so let's take Buster back to the Edelmans' and get on with it."

CHAPTER FORTY

While Andy and my father went out to hitch up the horses, Henry and I got Buster ready to go.

James watched as we all climbed into the wagon, Henry and my father in the front with Buster, Andy and me in the back with Spud. "Can't I come, too?" James asked, a bit defeated, which was unlike him.

"Here, come up here with us." I scooched back a bit to make room for him.

But when he clambered up onto the wagon bed, he sat alongside Andy instead, who gave me a startled look, same as the one I gave him.

I thought about James and his decision as we made our way toward the bottomland.

"How come you named your dog Spud?" James asked, his eyes on Andy.

Andy glanced at me quickly and away again. "I found

him in a trash can, when he was just born. You think he's small now, you should have seen him back then." He paused, smiling a little. "I let him sleep in bed with me, right up against my neck, and he'd tuck himself into a ball. Warm and tidy as a baked potato. So . . . Spud."

I pictured that. Was glad I could.

James said, "Would you have called him Carrot if he'd been long and skinny?"

"No, I don't believe so," Andy said. But he said it with a grin.

"How about Zucchini?" James rolled onto his knees and grabbed ahold of Andy's shoulder for balance as the wagon lurched over a bump. "Or Asparagus, and you could have called him Gus for short."

Which made Andy laugh. Something I hadn't heard him do for some time.

And I listened to that long after I couldn't hear it anymore.

When we reached the Edelman place, my father pulled up the horses and waited while Henry and I climbed down from the wagon, gathering Buster into the hammock of our locked arms.

"I'll get out here, too," Andy said, hopping down, Spud with him.

My daddy pulled something from his pocket. "For your

father." He held out some money, folded in two. "For Honk. It's not enough to cover the cost of her meat, but it's a start."

Andy looked at the money for a moment and then shook his head. "I'll be all right. He doesn't know where Honk went. And I've already paid for leaving the gate open." He touched his nose, which was still a bit swollen. "Keep that for her feed."

I watched as my father and Andy shared a long look. "If you're sure," my father said, putting the money back in his pocket.

And I found myself wondering if Andy was being up-right or just didn't want to explain to his parents how Honk had come to be in our barn.

But he could have just taken the money and told his parents nothing.

And he hadn't.

Despite everything I'd learned since the storm—mostly about how to balance things that tended to knock me off-kilter—I still felt like a scale. No matter what Andy did or didn't do, it seemed that the past—a sure thing—weighed more than the future: a might-be.

And I didn't much like how that felt anymore.

After my father and James pulled away, Andy and Henry and I carried Buster down the lane and through the big open doors to the barn, where we found Nora and her father, working with the dogs. Including a new one, a spaniel with a broken tail that dragged on the ground behind it.

"That'll happen when someone hits a dog just so, with a stick, say." Mr. Edelman shook his head. "Hell's too good for anyone who beats a dog."

He looked on as Henry and I laid Buster on a bale of hay. "And who's this?"

"I'm Annabelle's brother Henry." He stood up straight. "I know you didn't mean to hit my dog."

At which Mr. Edelman raised his eyebrows. "It was the other way around, boy, but you're right. It was an accident any way you look at it."

"Go on and get him settled in a pen with one of the others," Nora said, her hands on her hips. She looked better, her color good, some sparkle in her eye.

"But not with the bull," Mr. Edelman added. "I'm afraid he'll do some harm to any dog we put in with him."

Andy glanced at me. "Annabelle had him in her lap yesterday."

Nora gave me a startled look. "That terrier?"

I nodded. "I reckoned he was worth the risk."

"You're lucky you still have all your fingers," she said.

"No sign of Mr. Graf?" I asked.

Mr. Edelman made a face. "Who?"

"Mr. Graf. Remember? I told you about him. How he came looking for Zeus."

"The man from Aliquippa," he said, nodding.

"Who runs a pit," Andy said. "Which you already know, since you took him out of there."

But Mr. Edelman shook his head.

"If he came from a pit, he took himself out. I found him on the road, all banged up. But I never would have managed to get him into a cage if he hadn't been trailing a leash behind him and got it tangled in some brush." Mr. Edelman squinted at Andy, thin-lipped. "And how do you know about a dog pit in Aliquippa?"

"My father dragged me out there," Andy explained for the third time. "I didn't know where we were going. And I didn't watch."

I saw Mr. Edelman remind himself that this was the boy who had helped Nora. "I should hope not," he said with a little less edge to his voice.

"No, Mr. Graf hasn't come here," Nora replied, the sparkle gone from her eyes. "But it's only a matter of time."

Mr. Edelman sighed. "No sense worrying about something that hasn't happened yet. Until then, let's see if we can get Buster back on his feet."

Once he and Andy and Henry were busy settling Buster in the pen with the collie, I pulled Nora aside. "Would it be all right if I told Andy he could come over here and help with the dogs?"

Nora glared at me. "I thought you understood, Annabelle. This isn't meant to be a playground for wayward boys." She pursed her lips. "And I haven't forgotten what he did to your Toby."

"I haven't, either. But is every dog you bring here nice?"

She ran her hands through her yellow hair. "You can't blame them if they're a bit mean at first, after what they've been through."

I nodded. "When I found you lying here and I ran to Andy's for help, his mother slapped him so hard I could hear it from the porch. Just because *I* banged on the door and woke her up."

Nora drew her breath in sharply. "Why would she do that?"

"Same reason a person will hit a dog with a stick."

Nora watched Andy on the other side of the threshing floor, helping Henry unwrap Buster's bandages.

"I suppose," Nora said reluctantly, twisting her hands. "But if it doesn't work, he'll have to go."

"That's fair. And he might not even want to come. I don't know, really."

She looked at me closely. "You trying to mend him?"

"No. Though he mended me."

I told her how Andy had started my heart again.

"Well, why didn't you say so?" she said, her eyes gleaming. "In that case, he can come over whenever he wants. You tell him that."

"I've seen a dog with wheels hitched to his hindquarters," Mr. Edelman said later as we all stood outside the pen, watching Buster squirm, puppy-like, in his bed of straw. "Like a charioteer."

I pictured that. "Or maybe he'll recover, like Dr. Bloom said he might."

"Who's Dr. Bloom?" Andy asked.

"The animal doctor in Pittsburgh. He took Spud when the pound was going to put him down."

The look on Andy's face made me sorry I'd said it.

He dropped to one knee and put his forehead against Spud's. "*Put you down?*" he whispered.

"Maybe you can go see Dr. Bloom," I said. "Tell him how Spud's doing."

Andy stood up, blinking away his thoughts. "I've never been to Pittsburgh."

"It's not an hour from here!" Nora said.

Andy gave her a look. "Might as well be a million."

"But there's so much to see there!"

I raised an eyebrow. "I thought you said the city was a pepper grinder."

She shrugged at that. "Nothing's just one thing."

"I need to get home," Andy said. "I've already been away too long."

"But you'll come back?" Nora said, and I saw her father glance at her in surprise. "To help with the dogs?"

Andy seemed surprised, too. He glanced at the dog pens. "I might."

"Might's okay," she said.

Which was when the dogs suddenly began to bark, some of them rising to their feet, all of them looking toward the open doors of the barn.

CHAPTER FORTY-ONE

"I believe you have my dog," Mr. Graf said.

I was shocked to see him standing there in the door-way, a leash and collar in one hand, some kind of skinny club in the other.

He stopped just inside, across the threshing floor from where we stood.

Into the clamor of the upset dogs, I said quietly, "That's Mr. Graf. Come for Mudpie."

Mr. Edelman frowned at me. "Mudpie?"

"Zeus," Andy said. "She calls him Mudpie."

For that, I got a rare Edelman smile.

"And what dog might that be?" Mr. Edelman called, walking toward Mr. Graf, hushing the dogs as he went.

"His name is Zeus. Brown bull terrier. White splotch on his shoulder."

When Mr. Graf started toward us, Mr. Edelman held

up his hand. "I don't recall inviting you in, or onto our land, either."

Mr. Graf stopped. He looked startled, as if he wasn't accustomed to people telling him no.

"That's fine," he said. "I'll just take my dog and leave."

"And what makes you think your dog is here?"

"Your neighbor told me he might be. Mr. Woodberry, next farm over."

I glanced at Andy, who looked as startled as I was and shook his head *no, it wasn't me who told,* and I imagined that Mr. Graf had finally made his way to the Woodberry farm. I pictured Andy's father telling him to look here, where dogs were known to be.

Behind me, I heard a low rumble and turned to see Mudpie on his feet at the back of his pen, his eyes fixed on Mr. Graf.

I didn't need a lightning strike to know what that dog was feeling.

Nor did Spud, who cringed and whimpered at the sound.

Nor did Henry, who didn't know Mudpie the way I did but was already his.

Andy's face revealed almost nothing. But he planted his feet and kept his eyes on Mr. Graf.

Nora stood wiry and tense beside me, but there wasn't any tremble in her.

"Well, and there he is," Mr. Graf said as the growl reached him, smiling as he started again toward us.

"How much?" Nora called out. She hurried forward to join her father.

The other dogs had settled down some by now, but they were still on their feet, watching, muttering to each other, while Buster, who couldn't rise, whined in frustration.

"How much *what*?" Mr. Graf said.

"How much do you want for that dog?"

He shook his head. "He's not for sale."

"Of course he is. For a man like you, everything's for sale."

He clearly didn't like that. "A man like me?"

"How much?" she said again.

Her father said, "Nora—" but she waved him off.

When Mr. Graf took another step toward them, Mud-pie growled again, louder this time, his head lower, teeth like white thorns against his black lip.

"That bull is a goldmine." Mr. Graf walked closer. "If you offered me a thousand dollars, I'd have to think about it. But you won't, because you don't have a thousand dollars. And you don't have any way to stop me from taking what's mine." He held out the club. Two metal prongs protruded from the tip of it. "Do you know what this is?"

Andy swallowed hard. "It's a cattle prod."

Mr. Graf said, "So you know what it can do."

Andy nodded. "But you wouldn't use that on a dog."

Mr. Graf laughed a little. "Zeus is no dog. He's called a bull for good reason. Besides, he knows what this is. I won't even need to use it once he hears it coming."

Mr. Graf turned it on. I couldn't see a trigger, but he must have pressed one, for there was a sudden sizzling, snapping sound.

"You wouldn't use it on a person." Andy walked closer to Nora and her father, Spud at his feet.

"What does it do?" I asked, Henry close by my side.

"It gives a terrible shock," Andy said.

Nora stared at him. "Why would you want to shock a cow?"

"I wouldn't."

"This is getting tiresome." Mr. Graf took a few steps closer.

"There are five of us," I said. "You can't shock us all."

"No, but I can shock one of you." He looked at us in turn. "Who wants to be the one?"

"You wouldn't dare." Nora stood her ground, her father next to her, and I made up my mind that I would, too, though I confess that I was afraid of that club, the metal fangs sticking out from the end of it. What they could do to any one of us. Especially my little brother.

I clenched myself for what was coming.

But Mr. Graf surprised me. Without warning, he

started toward Andy, who instinctively backed away just as Mr. Graf reached down to scoop Spud into his arms and, running toward the other dogs, tossed him into Mudpie's pen.

"Spud!" Andy yelled, racing to the gate and yanking it open, rushing in as the big bull charged, snarling, toward Spud. And I screamed "No!" just as, once again, everything changed, and the bull swept past Spud and straight out through the open gate like a runaway train, thudding on the old floorboards, his nails scratching for purchase as he picked up speed—and made straight for Mr. Graf, who backed up but then raised the prod, ready for a fight.

"No!" I yelled as the dog launched himself at Mr. Graf's arm, gripping it in his terrible jaws and clamping down so hard that he swung from it, all four paws clear of the floor. The big man dropped the prod and tried to pull himself free, tumbling over backward, dust rising as the bull snarled and growled and shook his square block of a head while Mr. Graf yelled and rolled from side to side and pounded on the bull with his free fist, trying to break loose.

But that dog had been trained to hang on for dear life, and that's exactly what he did.

We all stood back, no way to help without getting hurt in the process, the dogs in their pens yelping and crying, Mudpie growling horribly as he sank his teeth deeper into Mr. Graf's arm, until I finally couldn't stand it anymore and grabbed the leash and collar from the straw, edging closer, Mr. Graf trying to scuttle away, his heels digging into the floor as he pounded on Mudpie's head, blood running down the dog's jaw.

"Annabelle, don't!" Nora yelled, her face so pale that the freckles on her cheeks stood out like a rash, her father holding her back.

"Wait," Andy cried. "Annabelle, wait!"

Which I did, which I had to do. There was no way to buckle the collar around Mudpie's neck, not when he was thrashing around as Mr. Graf fought him. Not as scared as I was. Nor strong enough.

"Lie still!" Andy yelled at Mr. Graf. "Play dead and he'll let go!"

Which seemed to make its way through the noise and commotion, though it must have been hard for Mr. Graf to go limp when the dog still had such a grip on him. When he had to be in such terrible pain.

We all watched as Mudpie unclamped his jaw after a long moment and backed away, shaking the blood from his face.

For a moment, I thought he might come after us, he was that worked up.

But he suddenly seemed to decide that he'd had enough—dropping his head, panting and drooling—and let us herd him into his pen.

I shut the gate quickly behind him and then knelt in the straw, shaking all over, while Andy picked Spud up in his arms and held him close.

I watched as Nora ran to the feed room and back again, her hands full of bandages, to where her father was holding Mr. Graf's damaged arm straight up in the air.

"There's no artery involved," Nora said, kneeling down and wrapping the wound tightly. "But you'll need stitches. Dr. Peck's closest. Just down the road."

I knew Nora could have done it herself. I understood why she didn't offer.

When she was done, Mr. Graf struggled to his feet, his face tight with pain.

What he did next shouldn't have surprised me. But it did.

CHAPTER FORTY-TWO

First, Mr. Graf picked up his hat, dusted it off against his thigh, and put it back on his head. Then he retrieved the cattle prod from where he'd dropped it and held it out in front of him.

"Clear off," he told us.

"You must be joking," Nora said.

Mr. Edelman almost laughed. "You think you can take that dog now, after what he just did to you?"

"Clear off!" Mr. Graf growled, sweeping the prod in an arc so we all backed away toward Mudpie's pen.

This time, Andy dropped Spud over the fence into the spaniel's pen, where Mr. Graf couldn't get at him. "There are still five of us and one of you," Andy said. "Same as before."

But he was wrong.

"Six." I walked to the pen where the big collie was watching, his eyes fixed on Mr. Graf.

"Seven," Henry said, dashing along to the pen that held the hound.

But Mr. Graf just laughed. "Good. I'm happy to take those other dogs, too," he said, cradling his bandaged arm against his chest. "I run through bait dogs like nobody's business. I can always use more."

I didn't need to ask what a bait dog was. I could imagine it well enough.

"Well, you can't have them," Henry said. "We won't let you."

"Then give me my dog back and we'll call it quits."

"You can't have him, either," I said.

The telephone lines were still down. No way to call the constable, even if I could make it past Mr. Graf. And, as my father had said, there was no law against dog fights anyway.

And probably no law against using a cattle prod on a dog, either. But there had to be a law against Mr. Graf using one on a person.

I went to Mudpie's pen and stood in front of the gate, my eyes on the prod, the sound of a thousand wasps rising in my memory.

"Go home, Mr. Graf," I said. "Please go home."

"Happy to. With Zeus in my truck. And I'll even leave these other mutts to you."

But I shook my head. We all did, as if we were one person.

I watched Mr. Graf look from Nora to Mr. Edelman, to Andy, to me.

I watched his eyes stop when he reached Henry, who stood not far from me. The smallest of us, now that Spud was out of reach.

I watched my brother stiffen, his hands curling into fists.

And I remembered what he'd said, about not wanting to fight Andy. Not wanting to fight at all. Not understanding the need for it.

The bull in the pen behind me knew a great deal about fighting. Had been taught to fight. Was good at it. Rewarded for it. Fought almost as a reflex.

Not so, Henry.

And I didn't know much myself.

But when Mr. Graf suddenly lunged at my brother, I threw myself between them, a sort of flying, sprawling, messy effort that nonetheless put me in the way, so when the prod found a target, it found me.

There weren't as many wasps this time.

But I was filled with a terrible burning pain where those metal prongs dug into my shoulder, and I was horrified by the look on Mr. Graf's face. How clear it was that he knew what he was doing. How he was deliberately pushing harder as I lay there, pinned down by the prod.

And then, just as Nora and her father and Henry all

reached for Mr. Graf, Andy grabbed me by the arm, and I saw his eyes widen as the shock passed through me and into his hand, felt him grip tighter, and remembered my father's voice, warning me never to do what Andy was doing.

And then it was over.

Mr. Graf lay flat on his back again, the others gathered around him, Mr. Edelman the one with the prod in his hand now, and I felt myself unclench a little.

There was a burning smell in the air, but I didn't realize it was me until Nora turned and gasped, her hands over her mouth. "You're burned! Annabelle, your shoulder."

I couldn't see it properly, but I could certainly feel it, and when I touched it gingerly with my fingertips, they came away red with blood that was seeping through the fabric of my shirt.

Henry helped me to my feet, his face full of worry, saying, "Are you all right, Annabelle?" as he'd said so many times since the storm had come charging through Wolf Hollow.

"I'm okay." Which was true, though my shoulder hurt quite a lot.

"You need a doctor," Andy said, plucking at my sleeve.

But when Mr. Graf stood up, clearly ready for what might come next, I said to him, "Before I go to the doctor so he can look after this burn, I will be talking to Constable

Oleska. And I'm sure he'll be stopping by to see you directly after that."

"You stole my dog," he said, still with too much anger in his voice. But I heard some worry now, too. Even some whine.

"I didn't," I replied. "No one did. Mr. Edelman found him on the roadside. He's nobody's dog. And you can't prove otherwise."

He flapped a hand toward Mudpie's pen. "That white splotch on his shoulder proves he's mine."

"And this burn on my shoulder proves something, too."

"I wouldn't have burned anyone! I was just trying to scare you. It's your own fault you got hurt."

I shrugged. "You can try saying as much, but we all know better."

He stared at me, and I could see a cold calculation in his eyes.

After a long moment, he said, "That dog, in exchange for an end to all this business? The dog stays here and you shut up about that?" He nodded at my shoulder.

"No," I said, surprising him.

"Then what?"

"Nothing. The dog stays where he is. You get on. I go to the constable."

The others watched in silence. Nora looked like she had something to say, but she kept her peace.

"And what's stopping me from coming back for what's mine?" Mr. Graf said. He seemed genuinely curious.

"You don't know me," I said. "You don't know my family. You don't know the Edelmans. And you don't know Andy," who glanced at me sharply.

Mr. Graf looked amused. "Is that meant to be some kind of threat?"

I shook my head. "Not at all. Just information." I turned and lifted the latch on the gate to Mudpie's pen. "We look after each other."

When I began to open the gate, Mr. Graf backed away. "Give me my prod and I'll go."

"Not a chance," Mr. Edelman said, tossing the prod into a far corner of Mudpie's pen.

And it was still there when Mr. Graf went out to his truck and drove away.

CHAPTER FORTY-THREE

The Edelmans wouldn't hear of us walking home, so Henry waited in their truck while I stayed behind for a moment outside the barn with Andy, who wanted a word before I went.

"I'm bigger than you," Andy said slowly. "And a lot stronger."

I didn't know what he was getting at. "What does that matter?" I winced as I pulled my shirt away from the burn on my shoulder, eager to get it patched up but more eager to hear what Andy was trying to say.

"You had to know you might get hurt, trying to put a collar on that bull." He looked puzzled. "And you knew you'd get a shock when you jumped in the way of that prod."

"And you ran into Mudpie's pen to save Spud," I said, equally puzzled.

Andy shook his head impatiently. "But you weren't afraid."

"Of course I was afraid! Good grief, Andy, I'm not an idiot."

"I didn't say you were." And there, the glare was back. But I was getting used to it. And I knew it didn't mean much.

"I'm only brave when I have to be," I said.

Andy sighed. "I can't remember the last time I was brave."

I gaped at him. "You saved an old cow and got a beating for it. You came with me to help Nora even though you knew you'd get in trouble. And you shared the shock from that cattle prod, not ten minutes ago!"

"The shock I got was nothing compared to yours. Besides, what I did? That's different."

"Why?"

"It just is."

I considered that, my chest hollow. "You also ran into a lightning storm to save my life."

Andy looked away. "That doesn't count, either."

"It does to me!"

"Annabelle, it wasn't like I made up my mind to help you. I didn't even stop to think about it."

"Which is the best proof there is. You didn't stop to worry about what might happen to you."

Andy bent down to scratch Spud between the ears. "Last year . . . that was the other side of the coin."

"I don't know what you mean." In truth, I did know. But I wanted him to say it. For both of us to hear it.

He stood up straight again. "I didn't think about what would happen to me in that lightning storm. But last year—that business with Betty—I didn't think about what would happen to you or anyone else. Including Betty. Including me. So I'm not sure it's a good idea: to do something without thinking it through."

I nodded. "Except thinking about something isn't the only way to know about it. And things don't always turn out the way you hope they will, no matter how much thinking you do."

He shrugged. "Even so."

Mr. Edelman called out to us from the truck, impatient to be on our way.

I waved with my good arm and took a step toward him. "You're really going home now?" I hated the thought of what might happen when Andy walked into his house.

He sighed. "I can't stay in your barn forever."

"Maybe you could live *here* for a while. Help Nora." I thought about Mr. Edelman. The work he'd left in the city. I imagined a greenhouse in the field behind the house. A cow grazing in the sunlight. "And help Mr. Edelman, too, with some planting."

Andy looked away. "I'm a bushel of rags and old hair, Annabelle."

I'd never heard anyone describe himself in such a way.

"Then stay here with Nora and become something else."

He had no answer to that.

"Was my father right?" I asked as I backed away, down the lane. "Do I remind you of things you'd rather forget? Or wish you hadn't done?"

Andy stood for quite some time, looking at his boots.

"You did," he finally said.

And then he turned and made his way toward home without another word.

But I kept the small one he'd given me.

CHAPTER FORTY-FOUR

My father was in the peaches when we pulled down the lane in Mr. Edelman's truck, Henry and I sitting on the tailgate, the big dog cage at our backs.

He came to meet us when we pulled up at the end of the orchard, his face stern.

I eased my way off the tailgate, trying to smile, my hand over my burn.

"What's wrong now?" he asked, his eyes on the truck.

"It's a long story," I said.

"Of course it is." He sighed.

"So this is the father of these remarkable children," Mr. Edelman said as he climbed out of the truck.

"John McBride." My father held out his hand.

"Gregor Edelman."

The two spent a moment sizing each other up.

"Gregor?" my father said.

Mr. Edelman raised an eyebrow. "You mean why not Gregory?"

My father smiled. "Not *why not*. I just don't know that I've ever met a Gregor before."

"After Mendel. The first geneticist." At the look on my daddy's face, he added, "My father was fascinated with the science, so he named me for his hero, and I eventually became a geneticist, too. Some seeds, planted early, are apt to bear fruit."

"You're talking about yourself, aren't you?" I said. "And how your father loved science and gave you a scientist's name—that's the seed part—which led you to be a scientist . . . and that's the fruit part."

Mr. Edelman chuckled. "As I said, remarkable children."

My father nodded. "I've been told about your other work. With the dogs."

If he'd meant to startle Mr. Edelman, he'd succeeded, and I expected to be scolded for betraying a trust.

"I didn't set out to tell anyone about the dogs or about Nora," I said to Mr. Edelman in a small voice. "Andy didn't know she was part of the secret, so he said something about her, and the rest came out, too."

Mr. Edelman gave me a rueful look. "We knew we couldn't keep that secret for very long, and it's Nora, more than me, who wants to put up fences." He glanced at my father. "You're about to hear a story you won't much like. Which is going to shine a pretty strong light on me and Nora and those dogs, so there's really no secret to keep. Not anymore."

"What story?" My father raised his eyebrows at me and Henry.

So I pulled my hand away from my burn and told him.

I didn't get far before he had hustled me into our truck and set out for Dr. Peck's, leaving Henry to explain to my mother why she should call the constable. Why he should meet us there.

"Annabelle!" my father said, his knuckles white on the wheel as he listened to the last of the story. "I feel like I'm in a twister, and you know how I feel about twisters."

"I'm sorry. We only meant to leave Buster with Nora and come straight home. We didn't expect all that other business to happen."

He gave me a stern look. Sighed a deep sigh.

"I suppose it's not your fault Mr. Graf showed up with a cattle prod. And I suppose I'd have done the same thing you did, putting yourself in front of Henry like that." He stiffened up again. "But when . . . well, I was going to say you might have taken a different tack with Mr. Graf when he offered that trade, but I guess I'd have done the same thing you did. No point in making deals with a man like that. And it would have been absolutely wrong to let him get away with what he did."

I watched my father soften.

"So, as a matter of fact . . ." He turned to look at me again. "I wish it had never happened at all, but since it did—" He smiled. "Well done."

But he wasn't smiling when we pulled up in front of Dr. Peck's and I pointed out Mr. Graf's truck, already there. "Come to have his dog bite looked after."

I watched my father cloud up again, like a sky before a storm.

But before the storm had a chance to break, the constable pulled up in his patrol car, and we spent some time with him on the porch, telling him what needed to be told, showing him my shoulder (which was an oozing and angry red), and making it clear that no one had stolen Mr. Graf's dog.

I tried not to worry too much about what might happen to the other dogs in the Edelmans' barn. Or what might happen to the Edelmans because of them.

I knew Constable Oleska pretty well. He liked animals about as much as anyone, and I reckoned he would turn a blind eye to the whole dog business, as long as no one came complaining to him, which seemed unlikely. If the villains who'd beaten their dogs cared enough to come looking for them, they wouldn't have beaten them in the first place.

Mudpie was different. Mr. Graf made a living off dogs like him.

"It doesn't seem right that dogs are getting killed in Mr. Graf's pit and he's making money from it," I said.

"Well, he *was*," the constable replied thoughtfully. "But the sheriff over in Aliquippa has been looking for a way to shut that pit down, and maybe now you've found one."

"You knew about the pit?" I was disappointed at the thought.

He nodded. "Not much we could do about it. No law against it, Annabelle. But there is a law against shocking people with a cattle prod."

"And is there a law against someone beating up a kid?" I said.

"Well, of course. Why do you ask? What kid?"

I glanced at my father, who nodded.

"Andy Woodberry," I said.

The constable frowned. "He admitted it to you?"

"He did," my father said, which was a surprise.

"When?" I said.

"This morning, after breakfast, when he was helping me hitch up the horses." My father took off his hat, ran his hand through his hair. "I asked him about it, and he told me. And he promised he'd let us know if it happened again."

"Which it will," I said. "Mr. Graf was at the Wood-berrys' earlier today, looking for Zeus. What do you think they'll do when they find out Andy could have had that re-ward? *Ten dollars?*"

My father began to look stormy again, surely feeling fond and maybe even a bit fierce about the boy who had saved my life.

We all turned at the sound of the door opening, the sight of Mr. Graf coming out of Dr. Peck's office, his arm wrapped in a fresh bandage.

I took my father's hand firmly in mine.

He looked down into my face and tried to smile. "It's all right. I know better." But I felt his anger, like a dark cur-rent through my hand and up my arm, and I was glad when the constable took Mr. Graf off to one side.

"You go on in and get that shoulder looked at," the con-stable said, but he was talking to my father as much as me. "I'll take care of Mr. Graf here. And I'll have a word with Andy, too. It'll be good to clean up both messes."

CHAPTER FORTY-FIVE

On the way home from Dr. Peck's, I worried out loud some more about what might be happening at the Woodberry farm, now that Andy had gone back home.

"Do you want to stop there?" my father asked.

"No, but maybe you should drop me at the Edelmans' instead. If Andy got in trouble again, he'd likely go there. Or maybe back to us."

My father drove on and soon pulled over to idle in the shade at the end of the Edelmans' lane. He turned in his seat to look straight at me. "Do you remember how you felt when you jumped between Henry and that cattle prod?" he said slowly.

"Of course I do. I don't think I'll ever forget it." A mixture of fear and anger and, well, love, certainly. Mostly love.

"Then just imagine how I feel at the idea of you in harm's way, Annabelle. Remember, always, that you have a responsibility to me, to your mother, to everyone in our family, to look after yourself properly. To think twice before you take risks. To consider what happens to the rest of us, every time something happens to you."

I looked at his kind, weather-beaten face and couldn't speak. Couldn't begin to tell him how much I loved him. How sorry I was for making him worry.

"I'll be careful," I said, blinking, my throat tight. "I promise I'll be careful."

"Good, then. Enough said." He gave me a look that was hard to interpret. Some calm acceptance. Some reluctance. Maybe a little sorrow mixed in. He cleared his throat and resettled his hat. "Do you want me to wait here?"

I shook my head. "I'll be all right."

"Well, don't take too long. I think your mother may be a trifle upset about Mr. Graf, and she'll want to see for herself that you're okay."

I climbed out of the truck. "Tell her a cattle prod isn't nearly as bad as lightning."

"I don't think I will," he replied. "In fact, I plan to stay out in the orchard for as long as I can."

After he'd gone, I crossed the gully and went straight out to the Edelmans' barn, not really expecting to find Andy there.

But when I reached the threshing room, I stopped

short, silenced by the sight of him sitting in the pen with Mudpie, Nora outside the gate, talking to them gently.

Spud, who was usually within inches of Andy, stood near Nora, eyes fixed on his boy and the big bull terrier on the other side of the fence.

I went on slowly, carefully, quietly saying, "It's me," from a distance so I wouldn't startle anyone, stopping alongside Nora and Spud but riveted by the sight of Andy and Mudpie sitting in the straw, Andy bowed down with his face cupped in his hands, Mudpie nearby, watching him.

Nora was saying things like "It will be all right. Everything's okay now."

And it was clear that she was talking to Andy and Mudpie both.

I imagined her on that train, kneeling alongside her dying mother, murmuring such things while chaos raged all around them.

But neither Andy nor Mudpie appeared to be listening.

Andy swayed forward and back a little, gently, like a rocker after someone has left it.

Mudpie glanced at me and then back at Andy.

And then the dog surprised me when he edged closer and laid a paw on Andy's leg, and I felt my heart notice.

Andy stopped rocking. At first, he kept his head down

and sat completely still. And then he slowly slid his hand toward that paw until he was almost touching Mudpie. Not quite.

It was the dog who did the rest, sniffing the back of Andy's hand, then his boots, the cuffs of his pants, surely harvesting whatever Andy had brought into the pen with him. The scent of Honk and Spud. Snot and tear-salt. Beetle carcasses and worm guts dredged in mud and pollen, crammed into his boot treads.

What Mudpie knew was different from what I knew. We each had our own truth. Trying to translate him would never make sense.

"Good boy," I said as he edged away again, settling in the straw, his eyes quite peaceful.

I slowly unlatched the gate. "Come out of there, Andy."

When he didn't respond, I let my voice harden up a bit. "Spud's worried about you. Come on, now."

At which he finally lifted his face and looked up at me, and I knew what had happened when he'd gone home.

He'd been punished again—his lip was split, his nostrils crusted with halos of dried blood—and I reckoned he had come looking for someone who might understand what it felt like to be in his shoes.

"You can stay with us," Nora said, her voice careful. "For as long as you want."

Andy looked from Spud to Nora and finally to me. "I'm sorry," he said, tears running down his ruined face.

"I know," I said. "But now it's time to move on."

CHAPTER FORTY-SIX

As it turned out, Andy decided to go back to the potato house for a while.

He told Nora, "If I still need a place to be when the potato crop comes in, I'll be grateful to sleep here, in the barn, with the dogs, until it's too cold. If you'll let me. And I'll work here all summer. I'm good at clearing ground," he told Mr. Edelman. "If you want to plant anything."

"All right," Nora said. "You come here to help with the dogs, and we'll pay you in food and pocket money."

"And I've been thinking about a greenhouse," Mr. Edelman said. "Just a small one. But I could use some help with that."

"I'll be working a bit at Annabelle's, too," Andy said. "Looking after Honk."

"That cow of yours?" Mr. Edelman thought about that. "She can come here if you like."

Andy hesitated. "I wouldn't want my father to see her. He'd try to take her back."

"To have her butchered?" Nora said. "For the meat?"

Andy nodded.

"Well, from a distance one cow looks much like another," Mr. Edelman said. "I think she'll be fine in the pasture back of the house."

Andy almost smiled but stopped when the split in his lip began to bleed. "I'm obliged," he said, dabbing at it with his finger.

Mr. Edelman sighed. "But isn't it more likely that your father will come to take *you* back?"

Andy shook his head firmly. "I told him I'd call the constable. And I will. I'm not going back there."

Mr. Edelman sighed. "All right. We'll cross that bridge when we come to it."

And he went off to look after the dogs.

"Come on," I said to Andy. "Let's go get Honk. And you can help explain to my mother how I got burned with a cattle prod." Although that would take a different kind of brave.

Once again, Andy and I walked along the bottomland, Spud between us, mostly quiet, down between the rows of field corn, our boots so clotted with damp earth that we had to stop often to kick them clean, until we reached Wheeler's

Run and, beyond it, the hill to home, and climbed the path together, companionable, easy, though I caught myself on the verge of saying, as we walked, that I was sorry about his battered face.

But I knew he would think that I pitied him, and I reckoned he was already working hard to smother his anger, so I didn't say anything.

Nor did my mother when we left our boots in the mudroom and went on into the kitchen, though she stopped cold when she saw him.

"First," she said, and she led me into the washroom to have a look at my shoulder, though there wasn't much to see except a square of white gauze taped neatly over my burn.

"I couldn't believe it when Henry told me." Her voice was as tight as her face. "*A cattle prod?*"

"Are you angry with me?" I was startled and on the way to hurt until she put her arms gently around me.

"*Of course not.* Henry said you were looking out for him. Though you might need to tell your brother that he's not to blame, Annabelle. I'm not sure he believed me. And I'm telling you the same thing now, that this was Mr. Graf's doing. His fault, not yours. But I hope you'll run if you ever see him again."

"Unless it's in a courtroom." Which shook her up all over again.

She walked me back out to the kitchen, where she

said, "And now you," and took Andy, this time, firmly by the hand and led him into the washroom to get cleaned up.

My grandma was sitting at the table, watching us go to and fro. "That boy needs looking after."

"He's getting some of that," I said quietly. "I'll tell you later."

And I went off to change into a fresh top.

When I came back downstairs, my mother was leading Andy out of the washroom, and his face was a clean pink, though his bruises were getting more colorful by the minute and one eye was edging toward swollen.

"You sit down here." My mother led him to a chair.

She poured him some lemonade.

"And you get on with those potatoes," she told me, which were steaming quietly in a bowl in the sink, cooked soft, waiting for someone to peel away their loosened skins. So I did that, dicing them into a second bowl, adding in a chopped onion, celery I had sliced into little green boats, boiled eggs I diced in the palm of my hand, mayonnaise whipped up with cream, salt, pepper, all of it folded carefully together so the potatoes would keep their cut, a bit of Hungarian paprika sprinkled on top.

I put the bowl on the table, added a platter of cold fried chicken, a bowl of dilly beans we'd canned the year before, a basket of warm rolls.

"What?" I said when I caught Andy watching me.

"Nothing at all." He looked sore and solemn but not quite as sad anymore.

"Then why don't you go on out and ring the bell."

No one, not even James, said a word about the condition of Andy's face when we all gathered at the table for lunch . . . though I caught my grandpap looking at him thoughtfully, and my father took him aside for a moment, to say something I couldn't quite hear. Something about the constable, I reckoned.

My mother poured coffee for the adults, and for Andy when he asked for it.

"Can I have some, too?" I asked, but my mother decided not to hear me.

"The Edelmans offered Honk a place to live," Andy told my father as we passed the dishes around. "So I'll take her down there this afternoon. But thank you for letting her stay the night."

My father shrugged. "You're welcome. Good to be able to do a thing like that if I can."

Andy nodded. "And if it's all right with you, I'll sleep in the potato house for a while longer. Until you need it for potatoes."

My grandpap put down his fork. "You're welcome to it."

It was clear that he had fewer *should*s than he'd had before.

My grandma smiled into her coffee cup.

And I was glad all over again that Aunt Lily ate her lunch at the post office.

"Can I go back down with you?" I asked Andy. "When you take Honk?"

Andy looked at me, startled. "Since when do you need my permission to do anything?"

"You're right. I don't." I turned to my mother. "Can I go back down to the Edelmans' for just a bit more? I'll do my chores as soon as I get home."

My mother drank her coffee, looking at Andy and me over the rim of her cup. "I suppose you can," she replied slowly.

And then I dished out strawberries with shortcake and whipped cream while my mother poured more coffee and Andy watched us do it, as if he were in some kind of school.

CHAPTER FORTY-SEVEN

It took some time for us to collect Honk from the pasture and lead her slowly up the lane and then over the top of the hill and down the other side into Wolf Hollow, the path at times almost too narrow for the big girl. Then we crossed Wheeler's Run where it ran wide and shallow, Honk picking her way, a little spooked by moments of sun shifting like gold lace on the surface of the water.

On the other side, she led us single file through the long, straight rows of corn and out again onto the road that ran through the bottomland.

"It would be easy to fix up the potato house," I said as we made our way toward the Edelmans', Honk clopping noisily on the stony road, swishing her long, tasseled tail at flies, tempted by the grass that grew along the verge but quite willing to be led by the boy she'd known her whole life.

"Fix up how?" He frowned. "It's fine the way it is."

"Oh, sure. If you're a rat."

He squinted at me, halfway to mad. "You calling me a rat?"

"I said *if*, Andy. *If* you were a rat, the potato house would be fine as it is. Or a mouse. Or a spider. But you're not."

We walked on for a bit. "Hay makes a nice bed, if it's stuffed into something," I said.

Andy plucked a leaf from a willow as we passed. "How would it be if I worried about me, and you worried about you."

I felt like I'd been pinched on the soft underside of my arm.

I stopped walking.

Andy went on for a bit before he noticed.

"What?" he said, looking back at me.

"Nothing," I said in the strongest voice I could manage. "But I think I'll go on home now."

We were only a few yards from the stand of trees that marked the edge of the Edelman farm, but I was suddenly eager for the things I knew through and through.

The chickens and their blowsy squabbles. The clatter of rock upon rock as I hoed a thirsty bean patch. The smell of hot soap and wet cellar stone as I helped my mother with the wash.

I missed sitting across from my grandma, knee to knee, my hands out in front of me while she wrapped them in yarn, loop by loop, telling me stories about her life. I missed James, who loved his Annabelle, though he had never once said as much. And my grandpap, who had told me so many stories that I thought of him as a great old book, the pages of him worn soft, closer now to his end than his beginning.

I had missed all of them—even Aunt Lily—for days now, while I chased things that danced beyond the tips of my fingers and left me breathless. Uncertain. Close to tears.

"What's wrong?" Andy asked, some of the gruff gone from his voice.

I decided on the truth. "It hurts to be around you. It hurts to be around you and want to be helpful and then feel stupid and small and useless for trying. So I think I'll go home now."

"Annabelle—"

"No, it's okay. You didn't ask for help. It's all right." I backed up a bit. "I don't want to sound like I'm boasting, Andy, but I'm luckier than you. Worrying about my own self is pretty easy. But if you don't want me to worry about you, I won't."

I'm not sure how Andy managed to look both annoyed and dismayed at the same time, but he did. "Good, then," he said.

"And I'm sorry."

"What for?" He looked baffled.

"You were pretty horrible last year—"

He stood up straight. "If that's an apology, I've heard better."

"I wasn't finished!"

"Then finish," he said, curt as a snap.

I ducked my head. "I used to think that what people do says almost everything about them."

Andy waited. "And now?"

I waved at a fly that had come for Honk and chosen me instead. "It's easy to see what a person does. But there's plenty more that's harder to see. And I don't think I was looking hard enough."

He watched me, his face serious. "And now?" he said again.

"Now I'm looking harder. I thought the lightning had made me smarter, and I suppose in some ways it did, just like books do, just like teachers do. All kinds of teachers. And they're all important. But I need to be my own lightning. My own book. My own teacher. I should have been looking harder all along. And I'm sorry that I didn't know what I didn't know."

He spent a moment on that, his eyes on my face. "About what?"

I gazed steadily back at him, though his bruises made me want to look away. "Everything."

And we went the last bit toward the Edelmans' together.

CHAPTER FORTY-EIGHT

We found Nora and her father in the barn, scrubbing away the last of Mr. Graf's blood.

"We've brought Honk." I stared at the stain on the floor. "She's in the pasture."

"Good," Mr. Edelman replied. "We'll bring her in here at night. She can keep the dogs company."

They both had every reason to look a little grim, given their task, but I could tell there was something else. "What's the matter?"

"Nora thinks we ought to put him down," Mr. Edelman said quietly, glancing at Mudpie. "And I'm afraid she's probably not wrong about that."

We all turned to look at the bull in his pen, at which he closed his mouth and sat up straight, unblinking.

"The way he attacked that man?" Nora shook her head.

"We could never trust him after that. And we couldn't in good conscience give him to anyone else."

"After you fought so hard to keep him?" I said, baffled.

Nora sighed. "Better to put him down than send him back to that pit." She peered at me. "I don't suppose you have some idea how he's feeling about all this? Something that might help us decide what to do with him?"

Andy watched curiously, waiting to hear what I would say.

It would have been easy to make something up. To say that I could feel how sorry Mudpie was for attacking Mr. Graf. That he wouldn't do it again. That all he wanted was a good home with good people and a chance to be a good dog.

But I wouldn't make Mudpie out to be something he wasn't.

And I wouldn't pretend to be something I wasn't, either. It was hard enough to know someone else. I didn't want it to be hard to know myself, too.

"I've lost that," I said. "It's gone now."

"Oh, my dear girl, I am sorry," Nora said, and I knew she meant it.

"I'm not sure I believed it in the first place," said Mr. Edelman, the scientist. "But I'm sorry, too."

"It's all right. I was lucky to have it at all. And it

wouldn't have helped with Mudpie anyway. He was always hard to read. Closed up. Private."

"Well, that was my last hope," Nora said. "That you'd find us a reason to give him another chance."

"But there is a reason," Andy protested. "You can't put him down. None of this is his fault."

"No, it's not." Mr. Edelman sighed. "But what's the alternative? Leave him locked up in a pen for the rest of his life? We rescue animals when they're treated like that."

"I'll take him," Andy said, but didn't sound too sure.

Mr. Edelman dragged his hand over his face. "None of it is Spud's fault, either. Are you willing to put him in harm's way?"

I watched Andy think it through. Watched him weighing things, adding a bit to one side of the scale, a bit to the other, trying to make it balance out.

"When he was told to fight, he fought," Andy finally said. "But then he fought the man who trained him to fight. Which makes me think he understands more than he's been taught."

We all thought about that for a while.

Then, "You'll look after him properly?" Nora said. "And you won't let him run loose?"

"If I can leave him in that pen when I need to, yes, I'll look after him properly."

Mr. Edelman nodded. "All right. We'll give it a try. But be careful. You won't know what he's about to do until he's done it."

I left Andy with the Edelmans and went home again, waving to my father and my grandpap and my brothers in the orchard as I passed by, trying not to care when I saw Hunter with them, trying not to care that I surely missed him more than he missed me.

"I can't understand animals anymore," I told my mother when I found her in the kitchen garden, weeding a row of eggplant.

She stopped and turned to face me. "You can't what?"

"I can't understand animals anymore. Not since yesterday."

"Oh, Annabelle." She dropped her hoe and folded me up in her arms. "I'm sorry." Then she held me away and looked into my face. "No wonder you've seemed so sad and, well, not quite yourself."

"Except I am myself. I'm back to what I was before. And that's fine."

She gave me a puzzled smile. "Annabelle, the girl you were before the storm isn't the girl you are now. For now and always, you'll be different because of what happened to you. Whether you can understand animals or not. Whether those lightning flowers leave scars or not. But that's true of everything that happens to you . . . and everything that happens because of you. Not just the big things, like lightning bolts. Everything, Annabelle."

She hugged me close again and then stepped away. "But be prepared for James to have a different point of view." She picked up her hoe. "He'll be sorry that your superpowers are gone."

As was I, despite the truth of what she'd said. Despite what I'd learned: that I had plenty, regardless.

I was lucky that way.

CHAPTER FORTY-NINE

Buster walked again before my burns had healed.

When he got up and staggered to meet Henry at the gate of his pen, my brother made a sound I'd never heard before, as if he were choking on his joy.

"Best thing I've seen in a while," Nora said as we watched the two of them, Buster walking like an old-timer but with plenty of puppy in his eyes.

"I bet your father's glad, too," I said.

She nodded. "He is indeed. He cried like a baby the night of that storm and again last night when Buster got up and walked on all fours."

I was a little surprised to hear it. I knew that Mr. Edelman wasn't nearly as gruff as he seemed, but I still had a hard time picturing him in tears.

"My mother would like to come down and see you," I said, careful not to look at her.

"What for?" she snapped, and I thought of feral cats, and Mudpie, and Andy.

"She was the reason I got to know Toby. She let me spend time with him. Else I'd never have known him at all."

Nora didn't say anything for a while. Then she cleared her throat and crossed her arms. "What does that have to do with me?"

"She's one of the best people I know. And I think she might suit you. That's all."

"We'll see," Nora said after a bit. Which was better than *no*.

And I remembered the feel of Mudpie's battered muzzle against my hair. How he had breathed me in. The choice he'd made.

"You seem better now," she said after a bit.

"Better than what? You mean all better after the lightning strike?"

She shook her head. "What happened to your friend. To Toby. You seemed to think that was your doing."

Which was part right. Part wrong. "Not my doing, exactly. But if I'd done something different, maybe he'd be standing on a hilltop right this minute."

She made a noise in her throat. "So you still feel that way?"

I shrugged. "Yes. Every little thing makes a difference some way or another. But I did my best at the time. It doesn't make much sense to fret about it now. Especially when I can't go back and do it over. Or undo it. Besides, there's plenty right here that needs doing."

"Such as?" She kept her eyes on Buster.

"Those dogs. The farm." I thought about everything that had happened since the storm. "People," I said. "They're a lot of work, too. So is being one."

Nora folded her arms on the top rail of Buster's pen. After a while, she said, "My mother was a terrible cook. Couldn't boil water." She paused. "I wouldn't mind learning how to bake a pie."

I gave her a thoughtful look. "My mother can bake a pie in her sleep."

"I thought maybe she could."

I decided to leave it at that.

I turned my attention back to Buster and Henry, who were now playing tug-o'-war with a bit of rope.

"Where's Mudpie?" I asked.

"With Andy. And Spud," she replied absently, her own thoughts elsewhere. "Same as always."

So I went looking for them.

For the first few days together, Andy had kept Mudpie on a leash while Spud was careful to stay beyond the big bull's reach.

From time to time, Andy would let the two dogs get

closer, Mudpie tied securely to a tree while Andy sat next to him and coaxed Spud near until all three were sitting together, Andy in the middle, one dog on each side.

So far, the dogs had touched noses twice, Spud quivering with nerves, Mudpie relaxed. The bull clearly knew that Spud was no threat, though I worried a bit about jealousy. As Mudpie began to trust Andy, I wondered if he'd want the boy all to himself.

But from what I could see, Andy had plenty for both dogs.

So I reckoned everything would be fine, if Mudpie could just see that for himself.

And if he could somehow manage never to confuse Andy with the people who'd come before him.

The test of all that came on the sixth day after Andy had taken Mudpie for his own.

Andy had been sleeping in the potato house, as planned, so I'd gone there looking and found him polishing the windows inside and out, the dust and debris all gone, two burlap sacks stuffed full of fresh, fragrant grasses, Spud napping up in a corner, Mudpie tied up outside in the shade.

"I brought you a strawberry pie." I held it out, a scrap of cloth over it to keep the flies away.

I imagined coming down to the potato house in the weeks ahead with other pies. Raspberry in July. Peach in

August. Apple in September. Pumpkin in October. Hickory nut in November.

Like a calendar.

Except the potatoes would come in before we reached fall.

"Thanks," he said.

There. Finally. The thanks I'd wanted and no longer needed.

He looked around for somewhere to put the pie.

I didn't say anything about bringing him a table. Or a chair. Or a bed.

He grinned at me, and I realized it was the first true grin he'd ever given me. "Why don't we just eat it?"

So we went out to sit side by side on the granite block that served as a step and, lacking forks, made tines of our fingers, scooping the pie into our mouths, until we had decorated ourselves with berry juice.

Then we took the dogs down to Wheeler's Run and washed up in the cool water, Spud splashing happily in the shallows, Mudpie watching eagerly from where we'd tied him, mostly healed but still scarred from all the fights he'd won.

When Spud clambered up the far bank and shook the water from his coat, I said, "Why don't you go on over with him, and I'll stay here with Mudpie and take off that leash, and we'll see what they do?"

Andy thought about that. "You think he'll be okay with Spud now?"

I looked at Andy, the shadows of bruises that lingered on his face, and, most of all, the doubt in his eyes.

"You're going to have to trust him some time."

He nodded. "But his name is Zeus. Not Mudpie."

"Why not Mudpie? Mr. Graf named him Zeus, which is an excellent reason to call him something else. And if you want him to be nicer, a sweet name like Mudpie works a lot better than a name like Zeus."

"Except he's *not* sweet," Andy said impatiently. "He's a mess, Annabelle. And you won't change that by changing his name. You can't erase what he was. You'll just confuse him. He's Zeus." He stopped and took a long breath. "But you were the first person who trusted him at all. If you think he'll be okay with Spud, I expect he will be."

I hadn't taken my eyes off Andy's face. "Spud will know better than either of us."

So Andy hopped the run from rock to rock and sat in the grass beside Spud, the two of them like brothers, as I spent a moment with Zeus, telling him what he needed to know.

And what I needed to know, too. What I should have known all along. And finally did.

"When you look at Andy, don't see anyone but him."

I bent down to unfasten the leash. "And when you look at Spud, see Spud."

I stepped back.

At first, the big bull stared at me in confusion, his head tipped, waiting for what came next.

And then he decided for himself, bounding into the water, kicking the sun from his paws, rolling in the cool creek water until I joined him there, Andy and Spud on their feet, watching.

And then, their minds made up, wading in.

When I walked back up out of Wolf Hollow that evening, I stopped at the top of the hill where the lightning had found me, near Toby's grave, the blue above slowly blushing to pink as someone tossed a fistful of swallows into the air.

I watched as the birds etched violet into the twilight, darting and soaring as if they were writing a poem in the sky, though I knew they were hunting. Trying to stay alive.

Two truths, one making a lie of the other.

Unless I believed them both.

So I decided to do just that.

And to keep my eyes open for more.

ACKNOWLEDGMENTS

Writing ought to be hard work.

It's supposed to demand whatever it needs to be interesting and compelling. And I have always relished the challenge of giving a novel what it needs. But the pandemic made everything harder.

I am therefore more grateful than ever for the patient and thoughtful support of my family, friends, and colleagues as I wrote and revised *My Own Lightning*.

I am especially grateful to those who weathered the pandemic alongside me: my husband, Richard; our sons, Cameron and Ryland; and Athena Gwendolyn Baptiste.

I thank my early readers, especially Suzanne Wolk, but also Mimi McConnell; Deirdre Callanan, Julie Lariviere, and the other Bass River Revisionists; Robert Nash; Patty Creighton; and Beatrice, Frieda, and Nancy Bilezikian.

For the endlessly evocative experiences I've had on their farm, I thank my grandparents, Ann and Fred McConnell. Likewise, I am grateful to my mother, Mimi, and my uncle Calvin McConnell for their stories about growing up on that land.

Although I don't know nearly enough about how dogs

see the world, I have learned a few things from the ones I've known best: Suzie, Snoopy, Lila, Tanner, Rascal, Dickens, and Spike.

I am indebted, as well, to Virginia Ryan Hoeck, who gave me a lovely and quiet week on Moosehead Lake in Greenville, Maine, so I could work on revisions in peace.

Profound thanks, as always, to my editor, Julie Strauss-Gabel, who understood and helped me cope with the fractures in my focus as I worked on this book. Her insights and instincts never fail to shed light where it's needed most.

I so appreciate the other members of my family at Penguin Young Readers, especially Jen Loja; Melissa Faulner, Rob Farren, and Natalie Vielkind at Dutton; marketing gurus Venessa Carson, Christina Colangelo, Andrea Cruise, Judith Huerta, Carmela Iaria, Trevor Ingerson, Bri Lockhart, Summer Ogata, Danielle Presley, and Rachel Wease; my publicist Kaitlin Kneafsey; designer Anna Booth; cover artist Dawn Cooper; Matie Argiropoulos with PRH Audio; and a boatload of amazing sales reps.

I'm running out of ways to thank Jodi Reamer, my agent at Writers House, who has enough spine for both of us and plenty of brain and heart, too. And her cohorts Cecilia de la Campa, Rey Lalaoui, Kassie Evashevski, Jessica Berger, and Alessandra Birch.

When COVID-19 put an end to in-person visits, I

learned to Zoom and was overwhelmed by the dedication of the many teachers, students, librarians, and readers of all ages who reached out to discuss *Wolf Hollow*, *Beyond the Bright Sea*, and especially *Echo Mountain*, which was released in April of 2020, just as the pandemic began to escalate. Books have always been bridges between us, but they have proven to be especially essential in recent years. My endless thanks to readers everywhere.

Finally, I am fortunate to have a wonderful extended family and a wide circle of extraordinary friends, too many to thank here, but all of whom deserve my gratitude . . . and have it.